REACHING HOPE

Dog Talk, Book 1

By

Joanne Jaytanie

Dedication

To all of you who have dedicated yourself to
protecting our country, I thank you.

Table of Contents

Acknowledgements

Editor Ruth Ross Saucier

Author Photo Samantha Panzera

Jacquolyn McMurray

The Baker Corp. has recruited Blair Sellick, a nationally known dog trainer with truly phenomenal skills, to provide exceptional training for service dogs. The project would provide highly intelligent animals as partners for victims of PTSD and other disabilities. Or would it?

The answer has disappeared along with Blair, her fellow dog trainers, and all the dogs.

Ex-SEAL and canine handler Zane Kelly is done with war, with dogs, and with Bolton's Soldiers. Coerced, cajoled, and eventually intrigued, Zane finally capitulates to Bolton's Soldiers recruiters for just one project, to find Blair Sellick. The mission is clear, the dog trainers are dying, and nobody has heard from Blair for weeks. Zane has failed only one mission, and that failure cost his canine partner Axel his life.

This time Zane has no intention of leaving anyone behind.

CHAPTER ONE

ZANE VAULTED OUT of his berth and landed with catlike stealth. He crouched down, slipped his hand between the mattress and the frame, and slid his Sig Sauer from its perch. The deck beneath his feet rocked gently. He waited for his eyes to adjust to the blackness; as they did, he glanced out the porthole to discover the early evening clouds now blocked all the stars. Slowly, a sliver of the crescent moon peaked from between the clouds, casting a glow over the water. He heard nothing except for the splash of the water tapping the hull of his boat. Nevertheless, his years of combat sent alerts vibrating through every nerve.

Soundlessly, Zane crept toward the stern. He'd left the hatch open when he went to bed, and now he inched as close as he dared to peek up toward the deck. Nothing unusual caught his eye, but his view was minimal. He retreated into the darkness and circled to the opposite side of the companionway and repeated the process. Zane couldn't identify the threat, but his internal imminent danger meter still pumped adrenaline. Someone was on his sailboat.

Easing himself onto the first rung, Zane glided up the ladder. The top half of his body cleared the companionway, and he immediately swept his gun around the deck. He halted when he located his target. The obscure figure sat on the far bench, legs stretched nearly the length of the bench and loosely crossed at the ankles. Not the typical posture of someone ready to attack, but Zane wasn't known for taking things for granted. He targeted his weapon center mass.

"You've got exactly two seconds to give me a reason not to shoot you," Zane threatened.

"You're a hard man to find, Zane Kelly," the faceless figure, backlit by the moon's glow reflecting off the water, said in a slow, relaxed manner.

"You're sitting here, so obviously not hard enough." Zane had left the ranch and escaped to his boat for a reason. Christ almighty. Was nothing off limit? He flipped up the safety on his Sig with a pop of his thumb. "How the hell did you find me?"

"Jamie."

"Son of a bitch, I knew telling him was a mistake," Zane snapped as he cleared the companionway and stood on the deck. Jamie would get a good ass-chewing next time Zane spoke to him.

"Your brother is worried about you. Jamie told me you dropped off the radar weeks ago. He wasn't sure you'd be here, but it was the only lead I had." The man hadn't so much as twitched, even with the gun still leveled at him.

That pissed off Zane even more. His lower jaw flexed and popped in and out, as if it had a mind of its own. He gripped his Sig so tightly his hand started to tingle. *I don't care who you are. One wrong move and you'll be fresh chum.*

"You can holster that damn thing. I'm not the enemy."

"Says you." Zane grunted. He lowered the weapon but didn't holster it. Where exactly did one put a loaded Sig when all you were wearing was your boxers? *Note to self, be sure to add an ankle holster under the mattress.*

Zane recognized the intruder's voice the first time he spoke. Nevertheless, he was so steamed that his brother outed him, he made certain the intruder got the point. "I'm in no mood to play twenty questions. Spit it out, Rob. Why the hell are you on my boat?"

"I'm here because I need your expertise. It's urgent or believe me I wouldn't have bothered," Rob said.

Rob Bolton, co-owner of Bolton's Soldiers, had tried to recruit him a dozen times before with no success. Zane was sure the guy had finally gotten the hint. And yet here he sat. Zane had always believed he'd have a lifelong career in the military, whether he was shipped home in a flag-draped box or forced out due to his age. His life had been charted out, and he knew his path until the day his military working dog, Axel, was severely injured on a mission.

When Zane was ordered home and told to leave

Axel behind, his plans changed. Bile rose up his esophagus like lava ready to rip the top off a mountain. His heartrate tripled and he sensed the start of his legs turning to rubber. Zane pinched his eyelids together, mentally forcing the physical reactions from his system. He wanted nothing more to do with the military or anything similar, and that included Rob's retired band of bleeding hearts.

"How many times do I need to say this? I'm. Not. Interested. Whatever it is you want, I'm not playing."

"Would you at least hear me out?"

Son of a bitch. Rob's self-preservation meter was busted for sure.

"If it's the only way to get you off my boat. Start talking." Zane sighed as he dug in a cooler for two bottles of beer. He turned and tossed one to Rob, who snatched it out of the air.

"Blair Sellick has disappeared. She worked as a contractor at a research facility owned by the Baker Corporation."

"Military?"

"Civilian." Rob turned in Zane's direction and dropped his feet to the deck. For only a heartbeat he hunched over ever so slightly and tucked his chin to his chest. "So far, nobody we've spoken to at the Baker Corporation will even admit to Blair ever being there."

"I thought Bolton's Soldiers only took contracts from the military and ex-military." Zane swallowed half his beer.

"Our network is global now," Rob said. "Doesn't matter who it is. If a request comes across our wires from past or current contacts, we check it out, and if we can help, we do."

Zane shrugged and stared out at the ocean. "Could be the woman had a change of plans. How'd you get wind of it?"

"A friend of mine is a private investigator and a college friend of Blair's. Mrs. Sellick, Blair's mom, contacted Molly the P.I. for guidance, and Molly referred her to us."

"Woman friend, huh. Let me guess. Molly's the college girl you dated. The one Jamie told me all about." Zane raised an eyebrow and shook his head. "And you're sure this isn't just her way to reconnect?"

"Hell no." Rob frowned. "Molly and I are still

friends. She wouldn't send someone to me unless the threat was real. Mrs. Sellick says Blair called at least twice a week. The last time Blair called, she told her mom she'd agreed to a transfer to a highly classified facility. The trainers were told the next stages of the program were top secret. Some cutting-edge concept and the Baker Corporation didn't want to take any risks with information getting out. Blair told her mom that she would call her after she got settled. Mrs. Sellick said Blair sounded excited about being one of the trainers invited to move to the next phase. However, two weeks with no contact means something's wrong."

"Has Mrs. Sellick tried to reach Blair?"

"Several times. Blair's phone keeps going to voice mail. Mrs. Sellick has also placed numerous calls to the company directly. She claims they are polite to her, but no one has provided her with any answers. Each time she calls, she's informed that all her messages were delivered promptly to Blair."

Zane stretched his legs across the deck. As far as he was concerned that still didn't confirm Blair was in any trouble. She could simply be too busy and forgot to call. Who calls their mother every week anyway?

"We've done our homework on this company, Zane. The original owner and CEO mysteriously died five months ago. Pete Baker purchased the corporation and renamed it in his honor. You ever heard of him?"

Zane shook his head.

"Pete has a colorful background. The Baker Corporation is his first legit company. He is, however, very well-known in the underworld. There's been rumblings about Baker going head-to-head with a mafia boss, and the mafia boss lost his."

"Yeah, but you guys deal with criminals all the time. You don't need me."

"Look. I know you've been through hell," Rob said. "But the best way to make it to the other side is to keep busy."

"I listened. You can leave now." Zane waved the empty bottle toward the dock. Sounds like the same bullshit he'd heard time and again since the day he walked away from the military. "Besides, you have a team of people and the cops on your side."

"We're overloaded. Everyone's on a project. And no one has your skills."

"Stop blowing sunshine up my ass, Rob. There are tons of retired military and capable civilians."

"We're particular. It takes a certain individual to be offered a spot with us."

"Then that settles it. I'm not asking. Go back to Sweet Valley, Texas, and leave me be."

"I'm not feeding you a line of crap. We need you, Zane. This is a special case. There's a reason we're coming to you—you were the SEAL's top canine handler. It comes naturally to you, interacting with dogs. And I promised Mrs. Sellick we'd locate Blair."

Zane scowled at Rob. "Dumbass. You know better. You don't make promises. And dogs? What do dogs have to do with this?"

Rob got up, crossed the deck, and sat on the bench next to Zane's chair. "The Baker Corporation selected ten top-shelf dog trainers to take part in a project. Blair told her mom she was one of the four trainers invited to continue. The six trainers removed from the Baker's project have disappeared.

Now even those selected to continue have vanished, so all ten are missing. Blair is said to be some sorta dog whisperer. She's known for her trainees' exceptional elevated ability, especially the dogs who help vets with PTSD.

"Bolton's Soldiers feel that is a worthy mission, and so should you. Whatever Baker is doing with these dogs and their trainers, you can lay odds it'll benefit nobody except Baker." Rob handed Zane a USB. "This contains everything we know about Baker's organization. Alive or dead, we've gotta find these trainers immediately. Just this one, Zane. And I promise, I'll never bother you again."

Rob's phone vibrated. "What's up?" he asked. "What! Ah hell. Yeah, I'll be heading back soon." He shoved his phone back in his pocket and looked Zane squarely in the eyes. "There's news. They found a trainer outside a bar owned by one of Baker's competitors. The trainer was mugged and shot in the head. Another was pulled out of Lake Murray, near San Diego and approximately four miles away from the Baker Corporation. You need to be our ears and eyes and figure out if the rest of the trainers are in danger. We still have eight missing trainers."

Zane's laser stare burned into Rob and he leaned toward the other man no more than an inch away. That inch wasn't to prove they were buddies. He made sure it was a blatant threat. He would do this for the dogs. He'd be damned that he would leave another dog behind. And he would do it for Blair. If training dogs was what she did, she was a person who needed to stick around. "This is your one and only ticket punch," he snarled. "When I finish this, I don't ever want to see or hear from you, or anyone else associated with Bolton's Soldiers."

CHAPTER TWO

BLAIR ENJOYED TRAINING a variety of breeds in large numbers much more than she imagined she would. On the trainers' first day at the San Diego company, Mr. Baker introduced them to sixty-three dogs. Their initial task was to spend time with each dog and grade them according to how likely the trainer would choose to work with them. During the month, Blair managed to spend time with every one of the dogs. Using her specialized technique, she sorted through them and weeded out those less willing to comply, whether it was due to lack of focus or unwillingness to work as a team.

The dogs were all between the ages of nine and eighteen months, and Blair was confident that they would mature to be good companions. However, based on the perimeters of the study, she only chose the dogs who instantly bonded with her. She was invited to participate in the study because of her track record, which was partially due to her remarkable rapport with dogs. She knew she walked a fine line. Blair didn't want anyone thinking she was a freak or cuckoo, which had happened before. What she could do with dogs...*hear* them, *speak* to them...she'd learned the hard way, was unique. All the trainers were being watched, so she tried to blend in.

Now with only four trainers left, Blair looked forward to getting to know one another, only that wasn't something Baker encouraged. Every trainer's room was on a different floor. They also had assigned assistants who kept them on schedule, which kept them apart. The assistants even told them what time to eat, and none of them ate at the same time. The only logical explanation Blair could come up with was that Mr. Baker didn't want them influencing each other. Even so, it felt like the walls of the building crept closer together with every sunrise.

A glacial caress skittered over Blair's bare shoulders. She grabbed the sweater from the open draw and pulled it over her head, rubbing her hands up and down her fleecy sleeves to warm both her hands and body. She was grateful her host had provided them with winter clothes. The temperature change from her home in San Francisco to the Baker Corporation in San Diego was doable. However, she wasn't informed they'd be going to the Colorado site and had arrived ill-prepared.

Walking closer to the window, she noticed the pane's outer edges were coated with frost. It brought back images of Christmas Eve when she and her mom cut out paper patterns and placed them on the cooling cookies' tops. They would sprinkle powdered sugar over the pattern-covered cookie, then remove the paper. Her mom would always say *each cookie was as unique as a snowflake.*

Blair's view encompassed the backside of the complex. The building snugged up to the edge of a wide-ranging ridge. There were immense evergreen trees, mountains, and lots of pristine snow as far as she could see. Colorado was a beautiful place, but Blair hadn't been allowed to step outside since they arrived over two weeks ago.

Turning back to the dresser, Blair reached for her purse. She was grateful she'd chosen her largest bag when she packed for this adventure. The bag was the only personal item she'd brought from the San Diego site and it had been inspected prior to entering the Colorado site. Blair opened her bag and brushed her fingers over its contents—some personal grooming items, including a lip balm she'd made. A tiny change purse that held a meager amount of bills, one debit card, her driver's license, and her favorite picture of her mom and her laughing. A token dog-training clicker, the invitation to join this program personally signed by Pete Baker, and a black velvet draw-string bag that contained some of her favorite crystals and gemstones. Lastly, a wooden, hand-carved, antique box that held ten bottles of essential oils.

Pulling the box out, she unlatched the lock and pulled out a bottle. It was a mixture of rosemary, lavender, lemon, and frankincense oils, along with a few more that she'd created to aid her with focus, creativity, and to manage tension. She opened the bottle and dabbed the oil behind her ears and on her wrists. Then she opened the velvet bag, and without looking, skimmed her fingers over the crystals until they lingered on one. Wrapping her hand around it, she lifted the crystal out and opened her hand.

"Hmm. I wonder what's in store for me today," Blair said as she stared at the shiny, black, obsidian laying in her palm. Obsidian is a protective stone. Commonly known to shield against emotional and physical negativity. It was also a good stone to help rid yourself of emotional blockage and promote clarity and strength. Her mother's worried voice floated into her thoughts. Blair needed to phone her mom and let her know she was okay.

A knock at her door drove her mom's voice away. She slid the obsidian into the pocket of her sweater. Time for breakfast; her growling stomach echoed her hunger.

Blair opened the door and greeted her assistant. "Morning. I understand Mr. Baker's concern regarding the possibility of someone leaking photos or exposing our research and his need to collect our phones. However, he did promise we would be allowed the opportunity to call home at least once a week. It's been over two weeks. I want to call my mother today."

"I'm sorry. That's not possible," the assistant said. "The landline came down during the last snowstorm. We're told that we're on the list for repair, however, it could be a couple of days."

Unconsciously, Blair rubbed her throat attempting to loosen the abrupt tightness. She bit her bottom lip, but quickly forced a smile as the assistant glanced over at her.

"GOOD MORNING," BAKER greeted them all.

Baker maintained a vast distance between himself and their group. He did not attempt to offer his hand or a smile. A wave of nausea roiled in Blair's stomach. Her heart rate increased, and her body temperature rose. His dark red aura was a clear indication of domineering tendencies and was so overpowering that Blair had honed into Baker's reactions to her group without forethought. He made a half-hearted attempt to sound friendly, but it came out sounding condescending to her ears.

Blair blinked her eyes to clear her head. She reached into her sweater pocket and rubbed the obsidian in an attempt to force the waves of emotional negativity away.

"As you can see, there are four groups of dogs," Baker said. "Each group is composed of the same breed. We're moving on to the next step of the study." He continued without acknowledging one of the trainer's raised hand. "Based on your results, sixteen dogs remain. You will train these top four from each of your lists. Your assignment over the next two days is to train your dogs to perform the specific tasks on this list."

Baker left the room. Blair and the other trainers read through their lists. The tasks were basic and comprised of behaviors she taught all her potential service dogs. They needed to retrieve a phone and bring it to her, locate a hiding person, open a door, alert her to a gas smell, turn on a light, and push her out of danger. By this point, she imagined that they would be tasked to begin training much more complex behaviors—and when were they going to learn about the next stages of this groundbreaking, top secret program?

Each group of dogs settled next to a spacious training area with everything the trainers were allowed to use. Blair had the four Dobermans and the other trainers had Malinois, Dutch shepherds, or Labradors. As she headed for the Dobermans, their stubs wagged wildly, and a couple stretched their bodies out across the floor trying to reach Blair without technically breaking their stay command. She laughed at their shenanigans, and they showered her with kisses as she reached them.

BY THE END of the second day, Blair was drained, but all her dogs could complete the list. She'd love some fresh air, but the trainers were not allowed to leave the facility. Not even to take the dogs out. Their assistants were in charge of that job. Their confinement constantly needled at her. As the trainers, they should be the ones in charge of taking their dogs outside. It would allow them more time and new surroundings in which to train them. Blair's thoughts continued to wander. She hazarded a glance up to the security camera, it turned slightly in her direction. Instantly she focused on the dogs as she shifted back and forth from one leg to the other. An itch tiptoed up one arm. The need to flee nearly overwhelmed her. A cold, wet nose poked her hand. She looked down, into the chocolate eyes of Hope's.

She smiled at Hope and rubbed her head. The contact grounded her. It did, however, prove she was right about the cameras. She'd become acutely aware that they were monitoring her more intensely, which probably explained the reason for her restlessness. No matter where she turned, a camera was nearby. She was afraid to say or do the wrong thing. Blair avoided eye contact with the other trainers and knew they felt, as she did, more like prisoners with each passing day. The stress was wearing her down and causing her dogs' tension. She now had a clearer understanding of what it would be like in Boot Camp. Their schedule was not their own. Every second of the day was planned out, with no deviations allowed. Her only haven was in her room. In the last few days, she'd made it a daily ritual to search the room top to bottom to make sure it remained camera free.

BAKER ENTERED THE training room, and everyone stopped what they were doing.

"You're getting new assignments. Tomorrow you will begin specialized training," Baker informed them.

"Aren't you going to test us on the first list?" one of the trainers asked.

"I already have," he answered.

Blair could swear the color drained from the woman's face. Of course, he knew exactly what they'd done. He'd watched their every move in the training room from the multitude of cameras.

Baker nodded at the employee beside him who handed out new training lists.

"You want us to teach the dogs how to steal a mock gun and a bag of pills? And how to distinguish between drugs and explosives?" another trainer asked. Blair sensed the bewilderment building within the trainer. She too was perplexed. Why would they need to train service dogs how to steal guns or search for pills?

"Is there a problem?" Baker inquired.

"Yes," the trainer answered. "I don't see how any of the items on this list is going to help a handicapped individual."

"Correct," Baker answered.

Baker's olive-green aura revealed his deep-seated malice. Like a neon sign, lemony-green streaks swirled upwards and bled throughout the room broadcasting his evasiveness. He was not a man accustomed to being questioned and anyone who dared risked facing his wrath.

"You said we were training the dogs to become service dogs."

"Exactly."

The trainer shook his head and frowned at Baker.

"Obviously, there was a miscommunication somewhere along the line," the trainer said. "I refuse to train a dog to steal drugs." The trainer crossed his arms over his chest and glared at Baker.

Baker looked at the employee beside him and gave the man a slight nod.

"This man will return you to your room so you

can pack your things. Be ready to leave here within the hour," Baker said with a dismissive glance.

The man gawked at Baker, then looked at Blair and the other two trainers. "Good luck," he said in a sarcastic tone as he left the room.

Baker is putting way too much pressure on us. At this rate the trainer left standing may have little to do with skill and more to do with perseverance. She wanted to cross her arms but knew Baker would interpret it as defiance. Instead, she jammed her fists in the back pockets of her jeans and willed her body to relax.

"From now on, each of you is responsible for feeding your dogs and taking them out. I want you to pick out one dog who will stay with you at all times, even to sleep in your quarters. You will all be escorted outside to the dog area now." Baker turned and left.

Baker is testing us; Blair was certain of it. He wanted to see if the dogs we chose outperformed the others, due to developing a closer bond. Picking out one dog was going to be difficult for her. She hated the idea of leaving the other three in the kennels at night. Could this also be part of Baker's test, to see how each of them reacted?

An employee appeared and escorted the trainers and their dogs to the fenced outside area. The trainers and dogs were allowed to leave the building only through the locked exterior door located on the backside of the kennel room which was connected to the training room. As Blair stepped out into the cold air, she inhaled deeply as if she'd just broken the water's surface and was sucking in a desperately needed breath. She said *okay* to the dogs, and they shot off into the yard.

Blair's overwhelming relief to be outside momentarily overshadowed her ability to see that the one-acre area was just another kind of prison. An eight-foot, chain-link fence enclosed the area. Even the top was fenced in, forming a box made of chain link. The only exit in the fence required a keycard to open. As she walked the yard, she took note of the cameras in groupings of two, each pointed in opposite directions and spaced every twenty feet. The sensation of being watched made her skin crawl. *Get a grip*, she scolded herself. She could leave at any time. Exactly like the other trainer did. Her stomach tightened and her jaw clenched.

Two hours later Blair had fed her dogs, taken them out again, then put them to bed. She chose the little red female she'd named Hope to be her constant companion. Blair had mentally reached Hope the first time they worked as a team. She wasn't sure if it was a strike against her, but she'd named all her dogs. It made it much easier for her to work with them, unlike her two colleagues, who called their dogs by numbers. She needed a personal connection to interact with them on a deeper level. She gave the other three dogs a rub on their heads, said goodnight, and took Hope with her. It nearly broke her heart when she looked into the sad eyes of the red boy she'd named Sin.

A KNOCK SOUNDED on the door. Since the first day the trainers took a dog to their rooms, their assistants had no longer escorted them, so Blair was surprised to find her assistant standing there.

"Good morning," said her former assistant. "Mr. Baker would like to speak with you." She led Blair and Hope to his office and knocked on the door.

"Enter," Blair heard Baker's muffled answer.

"Have a seat," Baker instructed without looking up. He studied his computer screen. "I find your methods both fascinating and infuriating."

Not knowing how to answer, Blair sat down, motioned Hope down, and said nothing.

Baker turned his screen toward her, and Blair saw herself.

"There," Baker said as he pointed. "Every other trainer uses virtually identical hand movements and voice commands. Everyone except you."

Blair stared wide-eyed at him. She'd grown to tolerate Baker's muddy red aura. Nonetheless, today it was so dark she could barely discriminate any red in its ambiguity. And being in such close proximity, the violent nature of his domineering and aggressive aura threatened to plunge her into blackness. Hope stirred at her feet. Blair slid her hands into her sweatshirt and rubbed the smooth red jasper. The stone was hailed for endurance, strength, and energy. Hope laid her head across Blair's feet and stilled.

"I'd like you to explain your small hand movements and your mannerisms. You never invade your dog's space. Mind telling me how you manage to get them to perform when you're not showing any dominance?"

Really? She thought. No matter her ability, she was sure her training method would not include the overbearing strategies she'd witnessed over the past seven weeks from the other trainers. She'd always gotten more results by allowing a dog options and rewarding only when the correct behavior was achieved.

"That's not my style," Blair said. "There have been situations when I've needed to take a stronger stand, but those are rare instances. By virtue of this project, we have strong bonds with the dogs remaining, and therefore, they should be responding to our training. We all had plenty of dogs to choose from. All along, you've instructed us to pick the ones we could best work with, have you not?" She only hoped she'd made her case without sounding like the babbling idiot she heard. Nevertheless, the last thing she'd do was tell him what really made her different.

Baker crossed his forearms and rested them on his desk. His dead, black eyes missed nothing. She waited. He studied her a moment longer, then slowly leaned back in his chair.

"I see. And if at the conclusion of the study, I decide you are my lead trainer, you would be able to teach the other trainers, correct?"

He was challenging her.

"Certainly."

"Good." He nodded. "Yours is the only name on my shortlist."

"And what is the job description?"

"To weaponize the dogs. They need to be solid in hostile situations."

Her fingers strangled the jasper. She prayed the stone's attributes would not fail her now.

"For the police departments and military?"

Blair bit her tongue to keep from yelping as her nails drilled into her thigh.

"No. My clientele is in the private sector."

"What kind of business?"

"The kind that uses guns and dogs to keep their

product safe. Good day, Blair."

If not for the adrenaline pumping through her system, her legs would've been jelly.

She stood, gave Hope a hand command, and forced herself not to sprint to the door. Baker was creating his own army, and he'd just designated her as the captain.

BLAIR AND HOPE joined the dogs and trainers already working. With the ever-growing intensity of the training, the trainers were on edge and short with their dogs. In turn, all the dogs were agitated. Stress filled the room, so Blair closed her eyes and sent calming feelings into the atmosphere. The two trainers blinked. Their shoulders relaxed, and the harsh lines on their faces vanished. Taking the lead from their trainers, the dogs settled down as well.

Now Blair finally knew the truth. They weren't going to help veterans or other disabled people at all. This wasn't the project she'd signed up to do. She and the others had been misled. No, they were lied to. She had no intention of training dogs to be used as weapons. And what exactly did Baker mean by product? Her eye twitched and her hands were clammy. Blair needed a plan to escape this place and to take the dogs with her. And she was certain asking to leave was no longer a possibility.

CHAPTER THREE

B LAIR AND HOPE established a behavior pattern between training sessions. After feeding all the dogs, everyone went to the outside area. When the group returned inside, Blair worked with each dog individually. Afterwards, she'd put Sin, Ace, and Dawn, back in their kennels, then Blair and Hope would walk the building. Blair continuously trained Hope. The employees greeted them if they passed in the hall, other than that, the two were ignored. Even though it appeared she was training Hope, the dog had become so attuned to Blair's psychic connection that Hope would perform with a single nod or eye contact. Their charade was so fine-tuned, it allowed Blair to focus on the employees in the halls and become familiar with their auras.

Blair tracked Baker's aura and knew he left the

facility between 7:00 and 9:00 p.m. That was also when the cameras in the training room were shut off. After he left for the evening, Blair waited for thirty to sixty minutes to take all the dogs out for the night. She timed it so she was the last trainer in the training room. The back room where the dogs were kenneled was left unlocked until 10:30 when an employee entered the room, checked to see all the dogs were in their kennels for the night, and locked the door.

On the training room side of the kennel room, the door had a keypad lock that didn't open until seven thirty in the morning. However, the kennel side of the door had no lock and could be opened at any time. Blair worked with Sin, the red male Doberman, until he could open his kennel door and then open the training room door. While Sin worked on his task, Blair projected calm into the other dogs' minds to keep them from barking or raising a ruckus. She praised Sin, gave him a couple of cookies, and then told him to return to his kennel. Once he returned safely inside, Blair gave each of the dogs a cookie for staying quiet. She said goodnight and closed the door behind her.

The part of Blair's plan that still caused her concern was getting out of the enclosed yard to freedom. That particular door needed a keycard. Over the past week, Blair had kept track of the employees and their keycards. She knew that only the seven employees responsible for checking on the dogs carried the cards to the external fence.

Blair overheard an employee telling a new guard that an extra keycard was stored on a hook inside the door to the employee's lounge. That same guard had also said that soon they wouldn't have to worry about carrying the cards, because at the beginning of next month they would be replaced with fingerprint locks. This update meant that Blair only had one more week before escape would be much tougher; manhandling guards and cutting off fingers were simply not viable options.

The employee lounge was rumored to be large and comfortable. Most of the employees retired to the lounge shortly after Mr. Baker left the facility. The only employees Blair ran across inside the building at night were a few cleaning people.

Outside was an entirely different situation. At least three guards walked the grounds at all times. Blair altered the times she took the dogs out for their last walk at night. Without fail, within twelve minutes of entering the yard, a guard showed up and walked the perimeter. Blair estimated that gave her eight to ten minutes to break out, reach the tree line, and follow it around the facility and down to the road.

Blair had worked out most of her plan and played it over and over in her mind. She would steal the keycard, go to the training room, and have Sin unlock the door to the kennel room. There was only one last piece of her escape plan to figure out. How to get all sixteen of the dogs out and across the open area before a guard saw them.

Blair and Hope took their afternoon walk around the facility. As they approached the employees' lounge, she noticed a note on the door. They slowed their pace and Blair read the note.

The lock company is coming out tomorrow. They'll be changing out the remaining keycards with fingerprint locks. Make sure to

*see me to schedule your meeting time with
them.*

Blair's hands turned icy and the chill ran up her
arms. She quickened her pace back to her room.

"This is it, Hope," Blair said after she shut and
locked her door. "We've run out of time. We must
make our move tonight. The problem is I haven't
worked out the last piece. We're going to have to
leave Sin, Ace, Dawn and the rest of the dogs
behind."

Hope whined and pawed at Blair. "I know.
Don't worry. I swear, I'm coming back here, and
I'm getting the rest of the dogs out."

BLAIR DRESSED IN layers to disguise what was under
her parka, gloves, boots, and scarf. She'd pulled on
her insulated long underwear, and extra layers of
clothing. She couldn't part with the antique box
filled with oils, her bag of crystals or the photo of
she and her mom. Blair shoved everything into the
pockets of her parka. She'd planned on collecting a
few things to take with them, such as food and water
for Hope, unfortunately they were being forced to

leave before she'd gathered any supplies.

Baker had stayed late, finally leaving at 9:10. Blair and Hope headed for the kennel room. She dressed the dogs the same as always in insulated snowsuit and boots.

Blair let the dogs out into the yard. One of the guards showed up, she smiled at him.

"Feels like a storm is blowing in." She continued her walk around the perimeter of the yard. Blair checked her watch. It was 10:00, and if she didn't want to risk running into an employee, she needed to get the dogs inside. She had to undress all the dogs, including Hope, to keep her from drawing attention. She put Ace, Sin, and Dawn in their kennels.

Blair and Hope walked down the hall as an employee headed toward them. She smiled at the person and didn't break her stride as she headed in the direction of her room. They arrived at the door to the employee lounge a minute later. Blair put Hope on a sit-stay and tiptoed up to the door. Reaching out with her mind, she tried to get a location of the employees. She homed in on the auras in the lounge. Someone was in the kitchen area. Blair stayed rooted and waited. The person got closer. They were directly on the other side of the door. Blair gave a quick hand-signal to Hope and the two ran to get around the far corner of the hallway.

"What?" the man at the door said. "Dammit, I'm on my way out. Fine. I'll do it. But I gotta get outta here in ten minutes."

The door closed and Blair gave Hope a stay signal and scurried back down the hall, again concentrating on auras. There was no one close. She placed her hand on the knob. Was she sure no one was behind the door? *Stop that. You've never been wrong before. Just do it!* Blair cracked the door open a tad. Quickly and silently, she pulled the keycard from its hook and ran back to where she'd left Hope.

The employee who'd gone to check on the dogs was returning down the hall to the lounge, so Blair froze and waited. The employee almost collided with another man as he opened the lounge door. He finally stepped through the doorway and walked down the hall, passing Blair's position without looking up. Blair's heart wanted to rocket out of her chest at that near miss. She held her breath as she waited for the woman who entered the lounge to realize the keycard was missing. She counted to ten and peeked down the hall. Not hearing any commotion or feeling any heightened emotions from the lounge, she and Hope headed for the kennel room.

Sin did not fail her; he opened the door to the kennel room so she and Hope could escape out into the fenced exercise area. It made her feel even worse about leaving Sin and the others. Maybe she could take all four of her Dobermans? "Stop this," she chided. "Sin, back in your kennel," she spoke gently. Blair rubbed Sin's chin and gave him a kiss on the head before she shut his kennel door.

"I'll be back. I promise I'll come back and take you home."

Sin, Dawn, and Ace whined softly. A tear trickled down Blair's cheek. She dressed Hope again and added an extra sweater under the snowsuit. She looked at her watch. According to the time she'd greeted a guard earlier, they needed to wait at least six minutes. Seven minutes later, Blair grabbed Hope's leash, clipped it to her harness, and opened the door to a snowstorm. This night was rapidly plummeting. She had no flashlight. It would be pitch black when they entered the treeline. Not only would they be trying to navigate the forest in the dark, now they had a blizzard to deal with. There was no choice. They had to make their escape.

She and Hope slipped through the training area and out the fence gate. Holding tightly to Hope's leash, the two began the run for freedom.

"Stop right there," a guard demanded.

How had the guard spotted them? No one should've been around for at least a few more minutes.

Blair mentally sent Hope a single word: *faster.* Without hesitation, Hope increased her pace, virtually dragging Blair. Snow slapped Blair's face. They were scant yards from the treeline; if only she could reach it, he couldn't shoot her through the trees.

"Stop, or I'll shoot the dog," the guard yelled.

Hope sped up. Blair kept running, gasping for breath. Her heart pounded in her ears. They reached the trees and burst through a thicket, when all of a sudden, another guard appeared, loomed over Blair, and tackled her to the ground. Eyes bulging, tremors engulfed every limb. She snapped her head to the side. Was Hope okay?

Hope lunged at the guard, grabbed his arm, and tugged at him, trying to pull him off.

"Hope, stop!" Blair screamed.

CHAPTER FOUR

"O FF," THE GUARD growled between clenched teeth in a hushed, commanding voice.

The guard had Blair pinned under him. Thick, black eyelashes framed his whiskey-colored eyes that glowed as he stared through his black balaclava, mere inches away from Hope.

Was he insane? Why would he think Hope would listen to him? Every taut millimeter of Hope vibrated as she maintained her clamp on his arm. The guard would be lucky if Hope lunged at him and only came away with the balaclava. But then, to Blair's utter shock, Hope obeyed his command and released his arm.

The guard sprang to his feet, still maintaining his grip on Hope's leash, and pulled Blair to her feet. Blair's heart slammed against her ribcage. She wasn't giving up now. She sucked in air trying to steady her breathing. The instant the guard loosened his grip she would alert Hope and they'd run. The muscles in her legs started to cramp. *No!* They were doomed. He'd drag them back and Blair would never see the dogs again.

He held her so close that Blair couldn't help but sense the impenetrable muscles of his chest, even through his parka.

"Run." The guard shoved her forward.

What kind of game was this guy playing?

"Why? So you can shoot Hope or me in the back?"

"If I were going to hurt the dog, it would have already happened," he snapped back. "And I've never shot anyone in the back, but if I had, it wouldn't be a woman."

The guard who'd ordered Blair to stop burst through the trees.

"Hell," the balaclava guard whispered, "too late."

The balaclava guard stepped directly in front of her. What on earth was this man doing? Was he trying to protect her? Her mind whirled as she sized up her situation.

"You caught them." The other guard barely got the words out as he wheezed. "They don't pay us enough for this kinda shit." He bent over and rested his hands on his thighs. "Gimme a sec, and I'll take them back."

Balaclava guard continued to hold Blair and Hope without flinching or responding. Blair felt his focus on her. She squinted at him; why was he staring at her? She slowed her thudding heart and locked her gaze on his, willing herself into his thoughts. The guard set his jaw and cocked his head slightly. Blair mentally pulled back, feeling a jolt of anger from him that vanished as swiftly as it had materialized.

Snail like, time crawled by until the first guard stood up, sucked in a huge breath, and walked toward them. He reached out and roughly grabbed Blair's arm, dragging her to him. Blair said nothing, refusing to give the brute the satisfaction of knowing he was hurting her.

"Get back out there and check the perimeter while I take this bitch back to the complex and lock up her and her damn dog." The guard huffed, still trying to slow his breathing.

Balaclava guard turned and ordered Hope, "Down." Hope dropped like a rock.

Blair glanced back, mentally pleading with the balaclava guard to help her. The next instant, balaclava spun around and kicked the guard squarely in the back, causing him to release her and sprawl face down in the snow.

Moaning, the guard reached for his holstered gun. Swiftly, balaclava pushed Blair out of the line of fire and leapt on the guard. He jammed his knee between the man's shoulder blades and shoved his face deeper into the snow. The guard abandoned the gun and sunk his hands into the snow, trying to gain leverage and push himself up. Not getting any traction, the guard flailed about, coughing and choking. Balaclava was relentless and never released the man. He held fast even after the guard stopped struggling under his weight. Balaclava zip tied the guard's wrists. He rolled the guard over and felt for a pulse.

"Is he dead?" Blair asked in a whispered voice.

"Not yet," he answered as he stood up.

"We need to—"

"Blair, we have to get out of here now." He pulled her away from the guard. "This place is going to be crawling with this guy's buddies any second now."

"How do you know my name?" Her eyebrows squished together as she frowned at the man. "Who are you, anyway?"

"Name's Zane Kelly. I was sent here by your mother to bring you home."

"Why should I believe you?"

"Your mother hasn't heard from you since the day you and the other three trainers were moved from San Diego." Zane reached down and patted Hope on the head. "Good girl," he said, handing Hope's lead to Blair.

"Then you know there are other trainers and dogs. We need to rescue them."

"That's not possible, we need more help and planning for that," Zane said. "Right now, my priority is you. But I promise I'll come back and get them after you are safe."

Flashlight beams skittered just short of where they stood.

"That's our cue," Zane said. "We need to leave. Now."

"Where are we going?"

"Away from here. Someplace I can keep you safe."

A surge of alarm tore through her. Her pulse beat the tempo of a snare drum in a rock band. Was she really going to go with this stranger? Hope nosed her gloved hand. She too realized it was their only option.

After what she'd just been through, anywhere was better than here. She nodded.

"Good," Zane said when she said nothing more. "Stay close to me. Let's go."

They moved as quickly as possible in the darkness. The sounds of their pursuers filled the night. The snow fell at a relentless pace and Zane kept to the trees for as long as possible, staying under their partial shelter. They could still hear the shouts of their stalkers, but their voices were tapering off as the trio quickened their stride and kept moving.

"We've run out of tree line," Zane said. "We need to move across the open space. The falling snow should obscure our tracks." He stopped and glanced back at her. "Stay in my tracks and don't look back or stop moving."

Blair gave Hope enough lead to be just short of Zane's heels. After hours of trekking through forest and downhill, they saw the lights of Aspen. Their clothes were soaked, and Blair fought to keep her teeth from chattering.

"My vehicle is over there." Zane pointed to the car sitting on the side of the road.

Blair hesitated before getting into the car. What were the odds that this man would be here on the same night she and Hope escaped? Too cold to think straight, she loaded Hope into the vehicle and settled herself on the seat. "Tell me you have a place for us to dry off and get some sleep?" She studied him from the corner of her eye.

"I do," Zane said. "This snowstorm is a blessing."

"Really? How so?" Blair asked, no longer able to stop her teeth from chattering. She pulled off her saturated gloves and rubbed her hands together in front of the dashboard heater.

"Not as many civilians around. Lack of visibility. Fewer cars on the roads. Which translates to fewer chances of being seen." He glanced over at her. "We're almost there."

They arrived at a hotel. Zane pulled around to the back of the building.

"You two go over to the back entrance. I'll meet you there. The fewer people that see us together, or you and Hope, the safer you'll be."

"Why are you going in the front? Someone will remember seeing you."

"The guard at Baker's may be able to describe me, so we can't count on staying here long. But the staff already saw me when I booked the room and expect me to be alone. Less interest, should someone come around asking questions."

ZANE WAITED AT the back door for Blair and Hope. He glanced at his watch for a third time. Eleven minutes had passed since he arrived. Where were they? He'd told them to meet him right here. He rubbed at his eyebrow, then ran his hand through his hair. Shit. He stomped his foot. How could he have lost them already? *You're getting sloppy, Kelly.* Zane walked out the door and headed toward the front of the hotel.

"Zane."

He heard Blair's voice and turned to see her and Hope coming up behind him.

"Where have you been?" He asked slightly gruffer than he meant to.

"There was a group of people standing around the back door when we first arrived," Blair said. "I walked Hope over to the bushes to let her potty and we waited."

Blair's lips were turning a light shade of blue, and Hope was holding up one of her front paws. Even with the booties, her feet were cold.

"Come on, the coast is clear. You two need to get inside and warm up." He opened the door and led them to his room. "You and Hope can have the far bed." That way, he was the barrier between them and the door. He turned on the shower. "Jump in the shower and warm up. I've got some dry clothes you can put on."

Blair came out of the bathroom wearing one of his flannel shirts and sweatpants; they were big enough for three of her. Her long dark hair was as wet as Hope's. She and Hope snuggled under the covers.

Zane's phone beeped and he grabbed it. "Shit!"

"What happened?" Blair asked.

He shook his head as he looked at his phone. He walked over to Blair and showed her the picture on his screen.

She gasped as she grabbed his phone and stared at the image. A tiny, strangled sound escaped from between her lips. Her eyes grew huge as she enlarged the picture on the phone.

"I take it you recognize him."

"Yes. He was one of the trainers." Chewing on her bottom lip she drew in a breath. "He voiced his opinion a few days ago about being misled regarding what we were doing, and Pete Baker sent him home. What happened to him?"

"Double-tap to the chest. They found his body on the other side of Aspen."

Blair's hand flew up to her mouth. She tried to stifle her moan. She wandered a couple steps back and forth, then stopped in front of him. Shaking her head, she looked into his eyes.

"Why would someone mug him?"

"He wasn't mugged. He was executed. Baker doesn't like loose ends." Her shoulders and neck tightened enough he could see her tendons stand out. "You have nothing to worry about, Blair. I'll get you and Hope back home safely."

"That appears to be a tall order with Baker on the loose." She handed him back his phone. "At one point, I thought about telling Mr. Baker I wanted to leave." She pointed at his phone with a shaky finger. "That could have been me."

"But you didn't. And now you're safe." Blair was beginning to panic. He'd seen these same signs too many times to count. Zane decided it was time to change the subject and deal with something he could actually fix.

"Are you hungry?" He walked over to the desk

and picked up a note pad and pen. "Here. Write down what you like to eat and anything special for Hope. While you're at it, put down a list of your sizes." She gave him a questioning stare. "You can't very well wear what you have on in public."

Zane left Blair and Hope locked inside his room with instructions not to open the door for anyone, no matter what.

ASPEN WAS OVERFLOWING with snow bunnies, hopping from pub to pub. It was the place to be in November. He hated the crowds but was grateful to blend into the flow of people. Zane was aware of every single person in his immediate vicinity for every second.

With it being so late he could only pick up a few things for Blair at one of the boutiques in a neighboring hotel that was running an all-night shop till you drop sale. He'd need to go out again tomorrow to collect the rest of the items on Blair's list along with the provisions he thought they'd need for the next twenty-four to forty-eight hours.

He opened the door to his room and was greeted by Hope. He'd nearly forgotten how much a dog could provide comfort. Her short tail whipped back and forth so quickly it was a blur. Zane gave her a rub on her head.

"Don't fret, Hope. I have food for you. I found a throw blanket and a belt that will keep you warm until tomorrow."

He dropped the bags on the desk and looked over at Blair. She was sound asleep and wrapped up in the covers along with extra blankets. Her straight, brandy-colored hair shimmered. She was stunning, both awake and asleep. He wished he'd met her when he was still in the military. It would've been great to have someone to train dogs with. Zane shook his head and closed his eyes. "Get a grip, Kelly," he mumbled between clenched teeth. If this were another time and another place, Blair would've been a woman who would spark his interest. But it wasn't, and she was his mission. He would get her home safely, and then he'd hoist anchor and sail somewhere no one could find him, not even his brother Jamie.

He and Hope ate and left Blair to sleep. He realized he'd been glancing at Blair every few minutes. If only they'd met two years ago. Why was it he'd never met someone like her when he was in the SEALS? He met tons of women, but all they were interested in was his status, what he could do for them, not him as a person. He needed to stop entertaining any notions about getting together with a woman. He was broken. And certain he would remain so. His scars were too deep and too raw to allow anyone into his life. Especially a woman whose life revolved around training dogs. He wouldn't go there again...he couldn't. Zane turned out the lights and stretched out on top of his bed, his ears alert to the sounds of the night.

CHAPTER FIVE

"GOOD MORNING," ZANE greeted Blair as he and Hope walked into the room. The atmosphere was so thick with worry it strangled him. He cleared his throat and aimed at sounding friendly. "I brought us a hot breakfast." Blair was leaning against the headboard, a death-grip on her pillows. He unhooked Hope and she ran over and jumped up on the bed. She sprawled over Blair's outstretched legs. He could see that Hope sensed Blair's distress by the way she was protecting Blair with her body. He raised a bag and tray of coffees. In his other hand he held a bunch of bags and topped it off with a smile. "And I picked up the rest of the things on your list, including an extra set of dry gear for Hope." Blair released the pillows and ran her hands down Hope's back. She looked up at him. Her gaze focusing and the haze of worry lifting.

"Great. I'm starved." Blair sucked in a deep breath as if she felt his comfort. "I'm sure Hope is too. I need to get her some food."

"Hope's been fed. I bought everything she needed yesterday."

"Thank you. I didn't even hear you come in last night. And thanks for the clothes." She smiled shyly at him.

Zane handed her a coffee, opened the bag, and pulled out a large Styrofoam container.

"I didn't know what you would want to eat, so there's a couple of choices."

"It doesn't look like the storm is going to stop anytime soon." Blair set her coffee down on the nightstand and took the container. "When are we heading back to rescue the dogs and trainers?"

"It's not safe for you, Blair. And we need more help to handle that many escapees. I'll get you home safe, and then I'll come back for everyone else after we have a plan and additional personnel."

Blair yanked her head back, scrunched her eyes

and frowned. He could see she planned to argue the point. Zane raised a hand to stop her. "I was hired to get you out and return you home safely to your mother. That's what I intend to do. I told you. I'll come back. I always do what I say I will. However, at the moment, you are my priority."

"My mother wouldn't want us to leave innocent people and dogs in danger. If she were here, she'd tell you the same."

"But she's not."

"We can't wait that long. Baker could move everyone again, and we'll never find them."

She had a good point. Zane had been thinking the same thing. He thought she'd continue to push her opinion. Instead, she waited.

"You make a good point. I have no doubt Baker will move what remains of your group. But we can't stay here. It's not secure. We need to get out of Aspen to someplace safer. It's not going to be easy. The weather's so damn bad I have no clue how far we'll be able to travel." Zane paced the room, there were no other options. He needed to implement the plan he'd come up with last night. "You and Hope stay here. I need to go find us a better vehicle."

BLAIR GLANCED AT the time on the television. It was only nine minutes later than the last time she'd checked. Where was Zane? He'd left hours ago, and she was beginning to worry that something terrible had happened to him. What if he didn't come back? What could she do? Where could she go?

She sat on Zane's bed, with her back to the door, and placed her hand on the phone. She needed to call her mom and make sure she was all right. Baker and his goons had no idea where she was, and there was no way he could trace every phone in Aspen. She figured it would be okay to phone her mom as long as she kept her call short. She picked up the receiver and read the instructions on the hotel phone.

The receiver was suddenly snatched from her hand, and she squealed in shock. Her sight narrowed as she fought off an overwhelming feeling of dizziness.

"What the hell do you think you're doing?" Zane asked her. He vibrated with anger. His aura flashed with red sparks magnifying his exasperation. "Are you trying to get caught?"

"I...where..." Blair cleared her throat and stared at him. "You scared the life out of me! Where were you? Why were you gone for so long? I thought something had happened to you." Her mouth went dry, she blinked rapidly to keep the tears from leaking out.

"And what? You were going to try and get yourself into trouble?"

"No...I...I was calling my mom. I'm worried about her. I figured if I kept the call short it would be okay. I want to make sure she's safe."

"Tell me this was the first time you picked up the phone?"

"It was. I promise. You told me not to leave the room. You said if someone saw us the probability of being found was high. You never told me I couldn't make a call."

She watched as the anger, or maybe it was fear, fell away from him. All the hard edges in his face softened. The transformation from scary to gorgeous was a bit unnerving. He scrutinized her. She could tell by the way his eyebrows pinched together that he was trying to decide whether or not to believe her.

"Okay. We'll get in touch with Rob Bolton and make sure your mom's safe. But we can't do that from here. We could be found. We'll do it from the road. I've got a couple burner phones in my gear. Let's get going."

"Rob Bolton? Who's that?"

"He's the guy that hired me to find you."

"You told me my mother hired you."

"I know. It was too much to go into at the time. Your mother reached out to Bolton's Soldiers via Molly, a college friend of yours. She's a P.I. now. Molly dated Rob when she was in college. Rob contacted me. Rob and I were special ops teammates."

"Ohhh, that's why his name kept needling at me. Molly called him Robbie."

Zane's mouth hitched up on one side. "Robbie? He's never going to live this one down." He chuckled. "Let's continue this conversation on the road." Zane squeezed his shoulder blades back, his head snapped back and forth. "Right now, we need to get out of here. I've had an itch all day that the wolves are hot on our trail."

"Where are we going?"

"I contacted a friend of mine. He's got a place off the grid where we can hide out. I'm just hoping the weather doesn't get any worse."

"Are we heading out in the morning?"

"That was the initial plan until this feeling of being hunted crept up on me. Let's pack up and head out now. We can be out of here in no time. With luck, we'll make it to our destination while it's still light."

Blair was dying to ask him where exactly he was taking them? Would they truly be safe? Based on the way he'd just gone from kidding around to all Military Man she figured it was best to keep these questions to herself.

"Is that everything?" Zane asked as he held the door open for Blair and Hope.

"That's it. We're ready…"

Blair stopped in mid-sentence as her eyes doubled in size and he heard the doors of the elevator open. Zane turned in the direction she was staring.

"Trouble," Zane confirmed.

Blair leaned closer to him and whispered. "That's Kevin. Baker's right-hand man. How did he find us?"

Zane closed the door quietly and led Blair and Hope away from the elevator to the back stairs and the rear door where their SUV was parked.

In the stairwell Zane said, "Take these." He shoved car keys into her hand. "Get down to the SUV, pull it out of the parking spot. Leave it idling and slide over to the passenger's seat."

"What about you?" She looked over her shoulder as Zane now pushed her toward the stairs.

"I'll be right behind you."

"But—"

"Go. Now." Zane returned to the hall and found Kevin running full speed, directly at him. Endorphins pumped throughout him, his system sucking them up like a kid eating candy. This was what he did. He relaxed his body and waited for the enemy to get nearer.

"Something I can help you with?" Zane asked in a lackadaisical manner. This was going to be a walk in the park. This guy operated on anger with no thinking involved.

"Get out of my way, shithead. I'm taking Blair and the dog with me, and it's gonna take more than you to stop me." Kevin's voice a gravelly threat. His arms ramrod straight. Hands balled into fists. Nostrils flared.

Kevin dove at him. Zane spun out of the way and barreled into Kevin's midsection, slamming him into the concrete wall and knocking the wind out of him. Kevin coughed and cursed as he struggled to regain his footing.

A door opened across the hall from Zane, and a man carrying a little girl stepped into the hall.

"You need to get back into your room," Zane demanded as he pushed the man back inside his room. "It's not safe out here."

The man started to argue but abruptly stopped.

"Watch out." The man pointed at Kevin. "Knife!" He slammed the door to his room. Zane heard the deadbolt jam into place.

Zane spun around and jumped to one side simultaneously. Kevin ran toward him, brandishing his knife. He missed Zane's arm by a hairsbreadth. Zane pivoted as Kevin turned and headed for him. The move gave Zane the chance he needed, offsetting Kevin, who held his knife in his far hand. Zane took the opportunity to kick him in the gut and hurled Kevin into the wall. Kevin's head bounced off the wall, like the ball hitting the sides of a pinball machine. He crumpled to the floor.

The door to the elevator opened and a bunch of people walked out. Zane fought the urge to run and loosened his stride. Once inside the stairwell he took the stairs four and five at a time, reaching the parking lot in seconds. He jumped into the SUV and peeled out of the lot, snow and slush flying in all directions and the backend fishtailing.

"Are you all right?" Blair asked as she grabbed the panic bar. She released one hand and reached out, running her hand over his arm closest to her and down his thigh as if searching for a wound.

"Not a scratch." Zane glanced at her and cocked up one side of his mouth.

"And Kevin?"

"Last time I saw him, he was lying on the floor unconscious."

Blair's blue eyes were twice their normal size and her eyebrows shot northward.

"No." She gawked at him. "Everyone was afraid of him. I heard he fights dirty."

"I'll remember that the next time we meet." He winked at her.

"You think there'll be a next time?"

"Always possible." Zane kept checking the rearview mirror, but he hadn't spotted anyone following them. "I think he was alone. No one's following us." He decreased his speed and blended in with traffic.

"How long will the drive be?"

"It's a few hours. But with this weather, it will take us longer."

A COUPLE HOURS later Hope sat up and started whining.

"She needs to go," Blair said. "We've been on the road for over two hours. Are we close?"

"About twenty more miles. We're coming up to the last good-sized town. We'll stop and walk her. Then head into a place to grab a bite to eat. After that, we should pick up more supplies. Once we get where we're going, I don't want us to leave until it's for good."

They had just ordered when Zane's phone vibrated. He pulled it free and read the screen.

"I need to take this," he said. "Kelly."

The waitress set the two coffees on the table, smiled sweetly at them, and walked away. Blair could feel the waitress study them. She needed to relax and act like she was enjoying herself. The last thing she wanted to do was give the waitress any reason for concern.

Blair forced her shoulders to relax and mentally shunned herself for chewing on the inside of her cheek—a dead giveaway of nerves. She stirred her coffee more times than the cook stirred the brownie batter. Her gaze darted around the room as she sipped from her cup, taking in their surroundings. She set the cup down and stroked the warm ceramic surface.

Zane reached out and covered her hand with his. She studied his hand and then glanced across the table at him. He smiled at her and leaned back. He was an impressive guy. He didn't raise his voice to the person on the call. Even so, the guttural vibration of his tone tickled the hairs on the back of her neck. It reminded her of the proverbial reaper of death crossing your path. In defiance of the timbre of his voice, he was leaning against the booth, shoulders at ease, legs stretched out and crossed at the ankles. The only tension he displayed was the fiery gaze locked on her eyes. The sensation ricochet throughout her entire body.

ZANE SENSED THE waitress sizing them up. Every nerve fired off when she'd hesitated after setting their coffee down. He didn't believe she was a threat, but even so the unwanted attention made him want to confront her. *Bad idea, Kelly.* Instead, he forced his body to relax. This wasn't a war zone, but they were being hunted. It was best all the way around for them to play the part of an ordinary couple stopping in for a bite to eat. He stretched his legs out even as every muscle fought to coil into an attack mode. As the final touch, he crossed his ankles all the while wrestling with his body's instincts to fight. Zane steeled his gaze on Blair. Unable to keep his focus fixed on her, he glanced across the diner and connected with the waitress's stare.

The spell was broken when Zane heard Rob's voice.

"Zane, are you there? I've been trying to reach you all day. What's your status?"

"We're heading to a safe house off the grid."

"You're not heading to Texas?"

"The weather is for shit here. Blair wants to go back and rescue the fifteen dogs and two other trainers."

"So, you got the picture I sent you," Rob confirmed. "That Baker is a heartless bastard. Tell me you're not heading back to try to rescue the whole crew?"

"I'm not heading back. At least not yet."

"Dammit all, Zane. Your mission was to pull out Blair and bring her back."

"I did pull her out. She doesn't want that jackass Baker to keep the dogs and kill the last two trainers. Don't worry, Rob. I'm doing this on my own. You guys don't owe me."

"That's not the point. Hold on a sec."

"He's pissed," Zane told Blair. "He's got me on hold. Probably bitching to his brother, Nic."

"Zane, please ask them to send someone to my mother."

"I will."

"Zane. You still there?" Rob asked.

"Yeah. But before you say anything, Blair is afraid for her mom. Think you could send someone out to check on her?"

"Already handled. Jamie kept harassing me to fill him in. I did. He knew we were short-handed, so he flew down to San Francisco yesterday and went to Mrs. Sellick's. She agreed to accompany him back to the Kelly Ranch and wait for your return."

That shouldn't have surprised Zane, but it did. For all the bitching he did about his brother, when it came down to it, Jamie always stepped up to help.

"Tell him thank you for me."

"I will. But it'd mean more comin' from you," Rob said. "I just discussed your situation with Nic. We're still short-handed, but we can be there to help you in a few days. Can you stay off the grid that long?"

"Yeah. I'll shut down my phone and pull the battery the second we disconnect. Next time we talk I'll use a burner. We'll work on a plan and keep our heads low." Zane heard Nic's voice in the background. He was urging his brother to make sure Zane kept himself and Blair safe.

"Zane. Nic just said that the storm is getting worse out there. I'm not sure where you are, but they're starting to shut down roads. You better get moving. Stay safe."

"Let's go." Zane stood up and tossed money on the table. "They're closing the roads. We need to get our supplies and head out."

CHAPTER SIX

I T WAS DARK by the time Zane turned off of the highway. He stopped the SUV and got out to put on snow chains. He jumped back into the driver's seat, pulled off his gloves, blew air into his cupped hands, and rubbed them together. The trio's SUV crept slowly up the narrow, unplowed, two-lane road. Their top speed was five miles an hour. The snow on the road was at least three feet deep, and he worried the SUV might get stuck at any moment. Blair had been silent since they'd turned.

Zane was glad he'd been to his buddy's place a few times before because there were no signs and no streetlights. Falling snow obscured their view even with the high beam of their headlights and showed no sign of slowing. He counted the switchbacks as they continued up the mountain. The next one should be the turn. At least he hoped to hell it was. With the volume of snow dumping on the road the SUV could get stuck in the blink of an eye. He cleared the switchback and saw the marker for the road. He exhaled as he turned and drove a mile out to his buddy's place.

"This is it." Zane told Blair as he rolled as close to the cabin as he was able. The SUV's headlights lit up the front of the place.

"Oh my gosh. The snow is piled up to the top of the porch railing," Blair said.

Zane popped open the center console and pulled out his Sig Sauer and flashlight.

"Blair, you and Hope stay put. There's a snow-blower in the barn. I'll clear a path up to the cabin and we can unload. Then I'll clear an area where we can take Hope to go to the bathroom."

"THIS IS A cozy cabin," Blair said. "Are there any neighbors close by?"

"No. That's why I picked this place. This cabin

sits smack in the middle of twenty-seven acres. The closest neighbor is miles away."

Blair kept an eye on Hope as she played in the snow while Zane made quick work of unpacking the SUV. After the trio made their last trip into the cabin, Zane locked the door and checked to confirm that all the windows were secured and locked. Blair put away the groceries and made them hot cocoa with a tad of Irish whiskey Zane pulled out of a cabinet.

They were sitting in front of the fire, enjoying their drinks. Blair was trying to relax, all the while the thought of Kevin or Baker's other goons played through her mind. Were they really safe here? Did they know who Zane was? Who his friends were? If they did, could they find this cabin? She closed her eyes tightly. She needed to shut down her train of thought. Zane was here, sitting in the oversized chair, his legs stretched over the ottoman, only a couple feet away.

Hope crawled up on the ottoman and squirmed her way until she was sharing his chair, resting her head on Zane's chest, and enjoying a head rub. He would keep them safe.

"Looks like you have a buddy." Blair smiled at the pair.

"SHE'S A GREAT dog and the first one I've been around in a long while." *Shit.* He hadn't meant to tell her that. Blair was too easy to talk to and he needed to keep his guard up if he didn't want her knowing the intimate details of his life.

He forced himself to focus only on Hope and not look over at Blair. He knew she was studying him. The atmosphere between them was thick with electricity. The hair on his arms stood up.

"Why did you leave the service?" she asked.

He glanced over at her. There was something very unusual about this woman; he could feel it. But he wasn't ready to tell her his story.

"It was time. We have more pressing matters to discuss. I want you to tell me everything you can from the moment you were employed by the Baker Corporation until I found you."

"GOOD MORNING," ZANE greeted Blair as she came out of her bedroom and headed for the kitchen. "Take a seat. I made breakfast."

"Coffee?" Blair asked as she pulled her mane back and wrapped a scrunchy around it. "I need to take Hope out." Hope was stretched out in front of the fireplace, and her head popped up when she heard her name.

"She's been out and fed," Zane said as he handed her a steaming mug and set a plate down.

"Thank you. But you don't need to keep taking care of Hope. You've done it for the entire four days we've been here. She's my responsibility."

"It's no problem. And you're both my responsibility. I told you, I don't want you or Hope going outside without me." Zane sat in the seat across from her. He was more at ease. She didn't have the impression of a coiled rattlesnake ready to strike. If she didn't know any better, she'd say he was even enjoying their time here. They talked, took walks, fixed meals, and played board games together.

"I don't want her to make you sad." She took a sip of coffee and looked over the top of her cup at him. "Sometimes, when you don't think I'm watching, I see the hurt in your eyes when you're petting Hope." Blair's mind was swimming in the whirlwind of sorrow and loss emanating from Zane. "You care for her, that much I know for certain, but I see your sadness all the same." She was forcing herself to breathe, clearing her mind, she centered herself.

Zane didn't move for a few heartbeats. Then he reached up, rubbed his chin, and frowned at her. "I've known a great many people in my life who are extremely sensitive to others, but you're different. I get the feeling you're gifted. Hypersensitive. Intuitive. You can sense people's feelings. You can communicate with dogs in a special way. I'll bet it's the same with all animals—maybe even with a touch of psychic energy."

Blair's fork slipped from her fingers before she could stop it. No one had ever noticed before. Not even her mother understood the feelings and emotions she could sense from others.

"What?" she croaked, at a loss for words.

He cocked his head and shook it. Rolling his eyes before he realized what he was doing.

"I don't do games." He rested his forearms on the table and leaned in, closing the distance between them. "I know there's something special about you, Blair Sellick. Why are you afraid to tell me? We've been together twenty-four seven for the last six days and you're still afraid to tell me."

"I'm not *afraid*." She sounded indignant, even to her ears. "I'm sorry," she said softly and lowered her gaze to the table. She played with the knife next to her plate.

Zane reached out and covered her hand.

"I won't tell anyone anything you tell me."

Her gaze traveled from his hand covering hers, up his well-muscled arm, and continued up to meet his eyes.

"I'll tell you. But only if you tell me why you walked away from the military." She was sure that would shut him down.

"Deal." His fierce whiskey gaze made her shudder.

"I've never told anyone about my abilities."

"Why?"

"Because I've never known anyone like me. I didn't want people to think I was weird, or worse, crazy." Her eyes darted around the room falling on anything but him. She licked her lips and continued. "I form a deep bond with animals, especially dogs. I can't remember a time when I didn't. When I was young, I thought everyone bonded the same way I do with animals. I asked Mom about it. She wrote it off to my imagination."

"But it's not only animals. I felt you in my mind the day you escaped the complex," Zane said.

"You did? I sensed your anger. My gift has changed and expanded as I've gotten older and used it more. I can pick up on emotions of both people and dogs. I also felt individual auras when I was inside the Baker Corporation. That's never happened before." She studied him. "If you could sense me in your mind, you must have psychic abilities too."

"It's just a sixth sense." Zane shrugged. "I can read people and animals. I've spent my life studying them. Because my life, and more importantly, that of my teammates depended on my ability to know how they would react."

"Hmm." Blair searched his face as if she would find the answer. "Keep fine-tuning your skill. I think you'll realize it's more." Blair relaxed in her chair. "Spill. I told you about my abilities. A deal's a deal."

"I was a K-9 handler in the SEALs. I completed hundreds of successful missions with my canine partner, Axel." Zane had the sensation of being crushed inside his own skin. He forced himself to take in a deep breath, then another. "We never left a man behind. We were deployed to Bosnia, a total hot zone." He wiped away the dampness on his forehead. "We were on a mission; I was retreating with the last hostage, who was just a kid, when we started taking fire. I heard a bullet whiz by and looked behind me to make sure Axel was on my six. He took the bullet and went down." His windpipe closed, he coughed, and cleared his throat.

Zane stared past her out the window, lost in the agonizing memory. "I handed the kid off to a team member in the chopper and turned to go retrieve Axel. Automatic weapons peppered the ground around us, but I was going to bring Axel home no matter what. I headed out to where I last saw him and got hit from behind, twice."

Blair gasped.

"I must've blacked out. I woke up a couple of days later in the hospital. They said I nearly bled out as I crawled toward Axel, even though I was ordered to turn back and leave him behind. I don't remember. They told me Axel was listed as KIA. But they didn't bring him home. They barely got me out. I spent months in red tape hitting dead end after dead end, trying to retrieve him. The military didn't stand behind me—they left my partner behind. A month later, when my enlistment was up, I walked away from everything I'd ever thought I wanted and got out." An icy shiver consumed him. He'd relived every second of that awful day. He was exhausted, like he'd trained for hours. His body and heart ached as it did the instant he woke in the hospital.

His mental barriers slipped, and a flood of raw pain and sadness filled him. It was Blair, her emotions bombarded his mind. He'd fought to keep that day pushed deep down inside. Until Blair came into his life and tugged at the gates that kept that terrible day locked away. Tears slid silently down her face. Zane leaned toward her and gently rubbed his thumb over one cheek. As he pulled his hand away, she took it with both of hers.

"I can't even imagine the feelings you've had to work through. I'm so sorry, Zane. I'm guessing that's why Bolton's Soldiers recruited you to come after me, because of your connection with dogs. I recognized it the first time you interacted with Hope." Her chin trembled, she bit at her bottom lip as she rubbed his hand with hers. Zane blinked. He couldn't distinguish where his pain ended and hers began it was so intertwined. "There aren't many people who have the natural ability you have to handle dogs."

"You do," he said in a husky whisper. The weight that had plagued him lifted. A sad smile creased her lips.

"Have you worked with Bolton's Soldiers before?"

"No. Rob and Nic Bolton were my teammates in the special forces. We've known each other for a long time. They'd been hounding me to join them, but I didn't want anything to do with the military. That included retired military. But Rob's like a dog with a bone when he sets his mind on something."

She smiled.

"He found me on my sailboat—the day before I planned to leave. Once again, I refused to get involved. Then he told me about the dogs. He knew that would sway me."

"I'm glad it did."

"Yeah. Me too. You're a good listener, Blair. Thank you." He'd watched her for too long. Zane needed to put some distance between them, he pulled back and stood up.

"More coffee?" He grabbed both mugs and headed for the counter. "We need a plan for getting the rest of the dogs and the trainers out."

"I've been thinking. I have a couple of contacts

in the FBI. I can get in touch with them, and you could tell them your first-hand experience. I don't know if there's enough evidence to link Baker to the murders, but I'm sure you could fill in the pieces of his connection to the mafia and drug-running." Zane handed her the mug.

"How long will all that take?"

"Could be a few weeks. Maybe more. It would keep you out of the direct line of fire."

"I've no problem telling the FBI anything I can that will help put that egotistical lunatic away—but after we rescue the dogs and trainers. You know as well as I do, with Baker's connections and money he could disappear at the first whiff of trouble. The more people who know what's going on, the more likely Baker will find out."

"You've got good instincts. But I don't want you putting yourself in danger."

"I got myself in this mess. I intend on getting the survivors out." She ran her hands through her hair, attempting to push back the pieces that had escaped from the scrunchy.

"What?" she asked at the strange, sad smile on

Zane's face.

"I wish I would've had you in my corner during my fight to bring Axel home. Maybe things would've turned out differently."

CHAPTER SEVEN

"JAMIE, IT'S ME. How are things on the ranch?" Zane asked.

"Everything's good here. I got Mrs. Sellick out quick enough to avoid being followed," Jamie said. "How are you two holding up?"

"We've kept our heads down. The blasted snow won't stop falling. Blair would like to speak to her mother."

"I'll put her on."

While Blair spoke with her mom, Zane dressed Hope for the weather, put on her harness, and took her out. It was peaceful out here. Zane felt more at ease than he had in a long while. The snow showed no sign of stopping. Fat flakes wafted in the air. Hope was sniffing the snow when suddenly her head snapped up. She stared out into the forest. The tree line was a half a mile away, and yet she kept staring. A low rumble started in her throat.

"What is it, girl?" he asked. She didn't look up; she scanned a small section of the tree line. "Is someone out there?" Hope's growling increased slightly in volume. She glanced up at him. "Let's go." Zane acted as if everything was fine as he and Hope returned into the house.

Once inside, he secured the door behind him, checked that all the windows were locked, and pulled down all the shades.

"I need to talk to Jamie. We have company," Zane said.

Blair stopped talking mid-sentence, and her jaw dropped open. Zane took the phone from her.

"Mrs. Sellick. Please put Jamie on the line. Now."

"What's up?" Jamie asked.

"We have company coming. Bud's got the outer perimeter wired. I've got the combo to his weapons stash. I'm not sure how many are out there. I can hold them down for a while, but I'm wondering if jumping in the SUV and leaving is the way to go."

"How fast are you going to be able to travel?"

"Ten to fifteen miles an hour if I want to stay on the road."

"Shit. You know they could nail you in minutes if they have sniper rifles," Jamie said. "I don't think you want to put Blair in that situation. Is there room for a chopper to land? Rob's crew has a chopper."

"They won't be able to land. There's too much damned snow. They'll have to perform a rope suspension rescue. Tell them to make sure they have a harness for the dog."

"Roger. I'm calling Rob. Stay on the line."

As Zane held on to the phone, he went into the bedroom and punched in the combo for the built-in wall safe. The door sprang open. It was crammed with M-4 rifles, handguns, grenades, a launcher, smoke bombs, a couple of helmets that stopped sniper rounds, and night vision goggles.

"Rob and Nic are heading to you, Zane. I gave them your location. They'll be there in seventy minutes," Jamie said.

"Okay. We'll stay put and hold our ground for as long as we can."

"Be safe, bro," Jamie said as Zane disconnected the call.

"My gosh. What does the guy who owns this place do?" Blair asked from behind Zane.

"Bud was one of my team members," Zane answered as he pulled out all the equipment he thought he'd need. "Any chance you can shoot?"

"I've never been close to a gun."

"Get Hope. I'm going to stow you two somewhere safe."

"What about you?" Blair asked.

The strangest sensation came over him. It was a feeling of fear and worry, but it wasn't his. It was Blair's. His eyebrows furrowed as he studied her. He stepped into her and cupped her chin, tilting her head up until she looked directly into his eyes. He felt the heat of her body. "Don't worry, Blair. I won't let them get near you."

"Hope," Blair called. Hope was by her side instantly.

"This way." Zane led them into the walk-in closet, reached behind a shelf, and pushed a button. A large piece of rug slid away, along with the floor.

"It's a safe room. You two get down there now."

"What about you?" Blair asked as panic filled her eyes.

"I'm going to hold off these bozos and then we're taking a helo out of here."

She took his face between her hands.

"Please. Don't get shot." Blair stood on her tippy toes and kissed him.

A foreign feeling engulfed him. It was so intense he was barely able to control the emotion. If not for his years of training kicking in, he was certain he would have succumbed. Now he understood passion. The sensation seared every nerve ending in his body.

Automatic gunfire ripped through the cabin.

CHAPTER EIGHT

"GO. NOW," ZANE ordered as he shoved Blair toward the stairs. Blair held tightly to Hope's collar and the two descended the stairs to the safe room. "No matter what you hear or what you think is happening, don't open this door. I'll let you out when it's safe."

Zane pushed the button and the floor of the cabin slid back into place. He took one last look at the closet floor and darted from the closet.

Another round of gunfire peppered the back side of the cabin, thudding into the thick wooden walls and spraying shards of glass from the shattering windows. The window shades were ripped away leaving exposed openings. He scooped up the duffle bag containing the weapons he'd gathered from the safe and headed for the main living area of the cabin.

The gunfire never let up as he slid along the wall and edged toward the windows trying to get a look at what he was dealing with. He could tell the intruders were getting closer to the cabin as the sound of the gunfire increased in volume. Zane could make out at least seven different shooters, but he was certain there were more. If he waited much longer the enemy would be safely inside the outer perimeter.

He was thankful he'd helped Bud rig up his defense system. Now was the time to cull the herd. He reached into his jeans pocket and pulled out a two-inch square black plastic box. Zane flipped one side with his thumb and exposed the red button. He peeked around the side of the closest window frame at the same time his thumb pushed the button. The blast was followed with the screams from the targets. Their screams gave way to silence, as the remaining mobile survivors scattered to find safety.

Zane crossed the room and hunkered down behind the huge oak log, one of the four that served as the four corners of the cabin. He slid the tip of his sniper rifle into the corner of the now wide-open space where a window had once stood. It was clear that the bulletproof glass Bud had planned on installing was still on his to-do list.

Using the rifle's scope, Zane surveyed the area he could see from his perch. Spotting movement, he focused on his target and pulled the trigger. A male voice bellowed in pain and the barrage of gunfire began again.

"Shit on a shingle," Zane grumbled under his breath. "How many idiots are out there?" He counted at least six shooters as he returned fire. All he had to do was hold down these jackasses for another—Zane glanced down at his wristwatch. "Ah hell," he snapped as he realized it would be at least another forty minutes before help arrived. Why did a clock take its damned sweet time dragging its feet whenever he was target practice?

Zane looked down at the loot he'd gathered in the duffle bag. He should have taken the launcher after all, but he didn't think they'd have an entire platoon gunning for him. He glanced back in the direction he'd come. Should he chance returning for the launcher? No. He'd have to make do with his first choices. Heading back would refocus the gunfire to the other side of the cabin. Blair and Hope might be in the safe room, but he'd be damned if he'd draw the gunplay in their direction. As he ducked to get a better look at his supplies, a bullet whizzed by. He felt the sear of the bullet as it ripped through the shoulder of his flannel shirt.

"Son of a bitch. It looks like I'm dealing with more than security guards." Could there be some special forces out there? He scooped up a few hand grenades. There were some smoke bombs alongside the grenades, he'd only use them if he had no other choice. He'd save them to use when the chopper arrived to help camouflage their retreat.

The gunfire had stopped—never a good sign. Zane slid back over to the corner, grabbed his rifle, and took a quick look through the scope. Just as he suspected. The intruders were making their way closer to the cabin. This would give him the opportunity to decrease their count one, maybe two, if he was lucky. He scanned the subtle movement. It should be like shooting ducks in a mudpuddle, except the damn snow had started to fall harder once again and he was having a difficult time pinpointing the targets.

Finally, he had one squarely in his sight. He had to take the shot, even if it meant only taking one of them out. Zane squeezed the trigger and the bullet hit its mark. An onslaught of bullets answered his shot. The intruders had covered a lot of ground and it would only be minutes until they infiltrated the cabin. Zane grabbed one of the grenades and hurled it in the spot where he'd last seen movement. The grenade exploded somewhere out in the snowstorm.

The wind had picked up as the snow fell and Zane's sight distance was decreasing by the minute. He picked up another grenade and froze. Was that sound the whirl of chopper blades or was it the wind playing tricks on him? Gunfire erupted once again, only this time they weren't hitting the cabin. The whirling sound intensified. Zane grabbed up the bag and rifle and sprinted back to the bedroom. He spotted Blair's bag laying on the floor. Without breaking stride, he scooped it up and shoved it into the duffle bag.

He dropped the bag at the doorway, ran over to the closet, yanked open the door, and slammed his palm on the button. The floor slid open. Backlit by the limited light in the safe room, Blair stood at the bottom of the stairs. Her legs were shoulder width apart and both her arms were stretched up and aimed at the top of the stairs as she held a death grip on a handgun. Hope was standing directly in front of Blair, right under her outstretched arms.

"Blair. Don't shoot. It's me." Zane made no sudden action, allowing Blair time to override her fight-or-flight mode. When she didn't so much as blink, he tried a new tactic and centered on her, flooding her mind with the message: *Blair you're safe, it's me.*

"Zane! Are you okay?" Blair asked without making a single move. "It sounds like a war zone out there. I thought you'd been hit, or worse."

"I'm fine. Would you lower the gun please?"

She blinked and fastened her gaze on her hands. A look of surprise spread over her features as she gawked dumbfounded at the gun she held. "I'm sorry," she said as she dropped her hands.

"I thought you said you'd never held a gun?"

"I hadn't until just now. I found it on the shelf. I guess survival instincts kicked in. I heard someone walking around up there. I don't even remember picking up the gun." Blair ran up the stairs and threw her arms around Zane's neck, hugging him fiercely. "I'm so glad you're not hurt."

"Give me the gun," Zane whispered into Blair's hair. He closed his eyes and inhaled her intoxicating scent before he pulled her away. Blair handed him the pistol and he took a quick look at it. The safety was off, and the pistol was loaded. He flipped the safety on and shoved it into the waistband of his jeans. "The helo is here. We need to get out while we still can. Put Hope on her leash, and you two stay glued to me."

Blair gasped as she followed Zane into the annihilation that was once a homey cabin. Snow was blowing through the shattered windows and starting to pile up inside the cabin. "How are they going to land a helicopter in all this snow?"

"They're not landing," Zane answered as he continued sweeping his sight and gun around them.

"You two stay right here behind this door. I'm going out to see what's happening." He didn't wait for Blair's answer as he melted into the storm.

Gunfire instantly erupted from the chopper above as a man enveloped in snow camo sprayed the treeline behind the cabin. Zane pointed his phone up at the helo, turned on the light, and was answered with two flashes. A packet was dropped a few feet from Zane. He snatched it up and ran back inside the cabin. Zane opened the packet, slipped into a harness, and then helped Blair into hers. He allowed Hope to sniff the K-9 harness and then gently slipped it on and secured her.

"Hope has never done anything like this," Blair said. Her face was as white as the falling snow. "I don't know if I'll be able to stay calm and get her on the helicopter."

"You only have to stay calm enough to get yourself into the chopper. I'll take care of Hope." Zane double checked the harness and then attached Hope's leash back on her collar. Blair's gaze ping-ponged around the remains of the cabin.

"Blair." Zane gave her a second but when she

didn't focus on him, he placed his hand on her chin, squatted down, and locked his stare on hers.

"Forget about the cabin. I'll take care of it. Right now, your only concern is getting out of here." She nodded her understanding. "Okay. The rope will be dropped as soon as we're under the chopper. I'm going to secure you and you'll be the first one to go up. But while I'm getting you snapped in, you need to hold on to Hope's leash. Understand?" She nodded once again, never breaking eye contact. Zane opened the door to the cabin and the man with the gun in the helo again peppered the ground.

"Ready?" Zane asked as he reached into the duffle bag and pulled out two smoke grenades. As if she were terrified her voice would betray her, Blair only nodded. Zane looped Hope's leash over his wrist and took Blair's hand. He flung both smoke grenades in the enemy's direction. The trio ran toward the hovering helicopter and a rope dropped down in front of them.

"Blair, take Hope." Blair grasped Hope's leash. Zane had Blair strapped in and ready to go in seconds. "Hold the rope right here." She handed back Hope's leash and did as instructed. Zane covered her hands with his, gave her a reassuring smile, and tugged on the rope. Blair rose into the air. At the same time, a second rope was dropped, and Zane secured himself.

"Hope, I know you've never done this before, but I'm an old pro. I can do this in my sleep." He snapped Hope into his harness and rubbed her head. "You don't have to worry. I'll take care of you." He wrapped one arm around Hope's body and gave his rope a sharp tug. He and Hope rose into the air. Gunfire came from somewhere behind them and Zane gathered Hope closer to him, shielding her with his body as the chopper began to move. The two flew, dangling in the air feet below the belly of the helicopter as the gunner strafed the source of the enemy gunfire. Minutes later Zane and Hope were pulled inside. The chopper climbed higher and raced south away from the cabin.

CHAPTER NINE

"**G**OOD GIRL, HOPE." Zane handed her to Blair and slid the door to the helo closed.

"Great to see you in one piece," Rob said as he slapped Zane on the back.

"Thanks for the rescue," Zane said.

"I take that back. What'd I tell you about playin' with guns?" Rob tugged on the blood soaked, ripped flannel shirt, and then looked down at Zane's leg. "Looks like you left behind a chunk of your thigh." Rob shook his head as he looked from Zane's thigh to his shoulder. "Son-of-a-bitch, Zane. You haven't learned a lick about staying out of the way of bullets." Rob chuckled at his own joke. "Drop your pants and lie down. Your thigh is my first priority. Then I'll get your shoulder fixed up."

As instructed, Zane dropped his pants and

stretched out on the floor of the helicopter. He looked up and winked as he saw Blair's cheeks turn pink.

"Yup. You got lucky. The bullet grazed the outside of your thigh." Rob dumped a solution over Zane's wound.

"Jesus, Rob," Zane hissed. "Sure you can't find something that burns more?"

"Stop being such a baby. Your wound should be stitched up. I'll wrap it up and do the job once we land."

"Got an extra parka?" Zane asked. "Blair is shivering."

Rob opened a compartment and pulled out two parkas along with a dog coat.

"We came prepared," Rob said. He tossed a coat to Zane and helped Blair with her parka, and then handed her the dog coat. "I gotta say, Zane. Watching you with Hope brought back memories of you and Axel. You reacted instinctively and the two of you worked together like it was simplicity itself." Rob focused his attention on Blair. "Zane and Axel were in high demand in their time. Our team spent half our time hauling his ass out to situations that needed him and his partner and the other half coverin' his butt. They were usually the first into a hot-zone and the last out. There was this one time…"

Zane moved up to the cockpit, in no mood to reminisce about his days with his best pal, Axel.

Nic told his passengers to buckle up and settle in, they would be arriving at their destination in a couple hours.

"Job well done," Nic said as Zane sat down. "Guess you'll be wanting your money and heading back to the ranch now."

"Hell no. I'm not done," Zane answered. "Blair's mom is safe with Jamie on the ranch, but I made a promise to Blair that we'd get the dogs and surviving trainers out of the Baker Corporation and I fully intend to keep my promise."

Nic glanced at Zane. "You've fulfilled your contract with us. Don't feel like you have to stay."

"It's not about the contract. It's about keeping my promise."

"I see." Nic studied him again. "Blair is more

than a contract to you, and I have to say, that's one helluva surprise." Nic's eyebrows drew tightly together. "Or is this about the dogs?"

"If you must know it *was* about the dogs. But somewhere along the line that changed. Now it's both." Zane didn't open up to many, but he and Nic had become close in their years in the SEALs. Nic had visited him every day while he was recovering from the injuries he sustained during the mission that had cost Axel his life.

Nic and Zane fell into a comfortable silence. Zane was at home in this environment. Until recently it was where he'd spent a lot of time. Rob and Blair chatted in the back as Hope stretched out over their feet and began to snore.

"There's the homestead." Nic nodded to the right. "Gotta say, I didn't think we'd ever get you out here. Unfortunately, most of the guys are gone. We've been flooded with contracts." He flipped on his mic and told Rob and Blair to prepare for landing.

"ARE YOUR ROOMS okay?" Nic asked as they

gathered in the situation room.

"Perfect, thank you," Blair answered as Zane pulled out her chair and then sat beside her.

"Zane, tell us about your plan," Rob said.

"At last count, there are fifteen dogs and two trainers still in the Baker facility." Zane gave them the rundown on the facility. "When we left there was already close to three feet of snow and it was coming down at a nasty pace. But according to the weather reports there will be a break in this pattern the day after tomorrow. If we don't leave tomorrow, we'll have to wait three days for another possible window."

Rob and Nic relaxed in their chairs seemingly comfortable with allowing Zane to take the lead.

"Our plan is to collect the fifteen crates here. We'll use the 400 size for the females and smaller males and the 500 size for the rest of the males. We'll need three Ford Transit 4x4 vans. All with the best snow tires on the market. Each van will easily accommodate five crates." Zane stopped to take a sip of his coffee.

"So, we outfit the vans here and caravan out to

Colorado." Rob picked up the lead.

"And each van will comfortably seat two people," Nic said. "That means easily a six-man team and a couple more can follow the vans if we think we'll need them."

"I'd say the fewer the people the better," Zane said. "Stealth is our best bet." Zane rubbed his chin as he thought. "Except we're going to need lots of hands getting those dogs moved."

"That's not entirely true," Blair jumped in. "I've worked with all the dogs for weeks and weeks. I'll only need one other person to help me get the dogs out of the facility and into the vans. It will only take us two trips."

"No," Rob said as he shook his head. "Our job was to bring you home. We have no intention of putting you back into danger." Damn him. Rob always wanted things done by-the-book, but only when it suited him.

Zane felt a flush of heat come over him as if he were ready to get into a fight, but he was totally relaxed—it had to be Blair. She was ready to set these guys straight, and if that didn't work, jump all over their shit. It made him smile. Without thinking he reached for her hand, and centering on her, he pushed a thought into her mind. *I've got you.*

"Rob, Blair's a grown woman and she's the only one that the dogs know and trust. I agree with her. She needs to be part of this mission," Zane said.

"What the hell are you thinking?" Rob snapped. "Tell 'em Nic. Blair's not going."

"Sorry, Rob. I'm with Zane and Blair on this," Nic said. "We won't stand a snowball's chance if we go in without her." Nic raised his hand as his brother tried to protest. "Fifteen dogs, Rob. Fifteen large dogs, we're not talking toy poodles."

And that's why Nic manages this place, thought Zane. He can see past today.

"Well holy hell," Rob hissed. "Fine. But if anything happens to Blair, you and Zane will be explaining to Mrs. Sellick. And just what do you think her reaction is going to be when you idiots tell her we had her daughter safely out, but we sent her back inside?" He folded his well-muscled arms over his chest, raised one eyebrow, and scowled at the other two men.

"Nothing's going to happen to me," Blair piped up. "I trust Zane. And if he says he's got my back, then I'm going." Blair mimicked Nic's hand raise to stop Rob. Zane could tell Rob was close to blowing a gasket.

"Let's move on, shall we?" Zane stared directly at Rob. "We have a limited amount of time to get this plan together and head out to Colorado. Baker could move those trainers and dogs at any minute."

"I don't think he will while the weather is so miserable," Blair said.

"It wouldn't be his first choice. But you can bet, if he's shoved into a corner, he'll do whatever he needs to do to keep his secrets," Zane said.

"You're right, Zane," Nic said. "And even though I want to be in the field with all of you, the more I think about it, I should stay here. We've got too many working contracts for both of us to leave headquarters for so long. And if something goes ass over tea kettle, I can be of greater help from here."

"We've decided to take the dogs to my family's ranch," Zane said. "We unload. Rob and your other three guys bring the trainers back here. Before you voice your protests, we have good reason for our decision. The Kelly ranch is completely fenced with sixteen-foot chain-link, topped with barbwire. We have the facility to house all the dogs and close working relationships with two top-notch veterinarians.

"Furthermore, Jamie has been closing ranks and has reached out to our special ops buddies. Five have already arrived in Washington. They helped my brother secure the ranch and are making sure no one gets anywhere near close enough to hurt Mrs. Sellick. We have several empty cabins on the ranch that once housed the ranch hands. Each of the guys have their own place."

CHAPTER TEN

THIRTEEN HOURS LATER, three fully loaded 4x4 vans pulled out of the front gate of Bolton's Soldiers compound and headed for Colorado. Zane and Blair's van led the way followed by Rob and three of his men. The snow slowly receded as the caravan crept across Texas and into the Oklahoma panhandle, but as they crossed the Colorado border it was back to whiteouts and snow-covered roads.

It was early evening the following day when they finally arrived at their destination. Based on Blair's descriptions of the inner workings of Baker's team at the facility, they'd decided it was best to wait until Pete Baker left for the day. The security team would do their rounds but tended to be lackadaisical when Baker wasn't on site.

Dusk was on the horizon. Rob was stationed

closed to the facility. He could see every person who came and left the building. He radioed the team to alert them that Baker had walked out of the facility.

"Let's hold for a few minutes after Baker clears our last checkpoint," Zane said. He was uneasy and that wasn't like him. Maybe having Blair go back into that devil's den wasn't such a great idea. He turned around to see if she was still asleep. Her eyes opened and she gave him a slight smile. "You sure you want to do this, Blair? I could take care of the dogs."

"I'm sure," Blair said as she sat up and rubbed her gloved hands up and down her thighs. "But you're still going in with me, right?"

"Of course. I'm your shadow no matter what." He reached out as she moved toward the front. She took his hand and held tightly to him as she stood close by. "Blair, I'm torn. I have no doubt you're the best one to get the dogs out. But part of me, an overpowering part, doesn't want you anywhere near that damn facility, Baker, or Kevin again."

"I get it, Zane. I feel the same way. But I must get the dogs. I promised them I'd be back for them and I'm keeping my word." Blair bent down and kissed Zane on his cheek. "It means everything to me that you stood up for me and convinced the Bolton brothers to allow me to be a part of this mission."

Zane reached out to pull her closer at the same time static sounded on his radio.

"Baker has cleared our checkpoint and is out of sight," Stan, one of Rob's contractors reported.

"Let's get this done," Rob said. "Converge on Zane's position. We'll roll in a little closer and set up for the infiltration."

Minutes later Ned, another contractor, hopped into the driver's seat of Zane's van. Rob, Stan, Hank, Zane, and Blair huddled in the back of the van and ran through the mission one last time. Ned and Hank jumped out and headed to the security building to incapacitate the guards and keep a lookout using cameras. Zane, Blair, and Rob would wait for Ned's signal and then the trio would enter through the front while Stan would keep watch on the vehicles and assist Rob, if needed.

"Lookout is ours." Came Ned's voice through

the radio. "Entrance is clear, you're good to go."

The trio rushed through the front door and Rob peeled off to locate and rescue the two remaining trainers. He would hand the trainers off to Stan and then Rob would go to Baker's office to search for anything that might be of interest.

Zane and Blair headed for the training room. Zane peeked around the last corner and gently pushed Blair back with his hand. She froze as he turned his head toward her, holding a finger up to his lips. She nodded and stayed quiet. As a guard walked by Zane lunged at the man, taking him down easily. Zane pulled the unconscious guard into an empty room and bound his hands and feet. Then he taped the man's mouth and grabbed his radio from his belt.

Zane went back to where he'd left Blair and rechecked the hall. They entered the large, dimly lit training room.

"The kennel room is over there." Blair pointed to the opposite side of the room and ran toward the door.

Stop. Zane's loud thought pushed into Blair's

mind. She turned and looked at him, her eyes wide with surprise.

"What's the matter?" she whispered as he reached her.

"You can't just rush in there," Zane murmured. "You have no idea if anyone is inside."

"I've already checked. Sin knows we're here. There's no one with them," she told Zane.

"You can really talk to animals?" Zane asked in amazement.

"Not exactly. It's more like I can feel their moods and emotions. And as with Hope, Sin and I are closely connected. He's excited I'm here."

"Okay. Then let's go."

As Blair opened the door, the big red Doberman male jumped up and down in front of her. "Hi, Sin. I'm so happy to see you." Sin whined and licked Blair's hands and face as she squatted down to greet him.

"They leave him out?" Zane asked.

"No. I taught him how to get out of his crate."

"Good to know," Zane said. He pulled out his radio and contacted Stan. "We're ready for the first load."

"Roger, vans in place," Stan responded.

"Let's take Sin last. He's a good lookout," Zane said.

Blair leashed up the four Malinois and Dutch shepherds while Zane went out into the fenced-in dog area and double-checked that their escape route was still clear. He radioed Ned to inform him that they were ready to go and the electronic lock on the gate released. He opened the kennel room door and Blair handed him the leads of the Malinois and they headed for the vans.

Between the three of them they got the eight dogs quickly loaded. Zane and Blair headed back to the facility. Blair was putting a coat on Dawn when they heard a noise out in the training room. Blair froze, only her eyes moved as she looked up at Zane.

"Keep getting them ready to go," Zane whispered as he headed for the door. "I'll go check it out."

Zane walked toward the training room. As he entered, someone shoved him into the wall.

"I had a feeling there was a damned rat in here,"

Kevin snarled as he lunged at Zane. Zane pivoted into Kevin and landed a kick in his groin. "Shit head. You're a dead man," Kevin seethed with rage. "You're not making it out of here alive."

"Yeah, yeah. Like I haven't heard that one before," Zane taunted Kevin. "I've had better men than you tell me that. Bring it on, asshat."

Kevin growled like a pissed-off bear and charged at him. He punched Zane squarely in the gut and went in for a second shot.

BLAIR WAS SECURING Ace's coat as she heard the rage in Kevin's voice. She never liked the guy much, but the tone in his voice sent chills down her. She tiptoed over to the training room door and pushed it open a crack so she could see what was happening.

The two men were throwing punch after punch at each other. Zane kicked Kevin in the chest throwing the man off balance. Except instead of staying down, Kevin sprang to his feet, his face a mask of outrage. He didn't look human. He punched Zane in the kidney and Blair gasped, causing Zane to look in her direction.

Get the dogs, Blair. Leave.

The words in her mind were as clear as if he'd said them out loud. Blair covered her mouth to keep from crying out. She blinked rapidly as she saw a flash of metal. She tried to yell out to warn Zane, only her voice wouldn't come. *Knife!* Blair forced the single word into Zane's mind.

Zane broke eye contact with Blair and refocused on his enemy. It was a heartbeat too late. Kevin slashed out with the knife and sliced Zane's forearm. Zane jumped back as Kevin descended on him. Before Blair realized what was happening, Sin rammed his body through the door and ran into the training room. At full stride Sin rocketed into the air and slammed his body into Kevin's upper back, driving Kevin down. Kevin's knife fell free and skittered away as his face smashed into the floor, knocking him out cold. Sin sat down directly in front of Zane.

"Good boy, Sin," Zane praised the dog and

rubbed under Sin's chin. He picked up the knife and shoved it into his back pocket as they walked past the sprawled Kevin.

"Thanks for sending out the assist," Zane said.

"I didn't send Sin." Blair shook her head. "He barreled past me."

"Huh." He rubbed Sin's head and smiled at the dog. "Let's get out of here before Kevin comes to, or someone else shows up."

Blair handed Zane three of the Labradors. She took one Lab and the three Dobermans.

They left the building and headed for the vans. Two of the vehicles were idling a few feet in front of the third. When Rob saw them approaching, he threw open the side door, hopped into the driver's seat and started the third van. Blair got into the back of the van and loaded the dogs as Zane handed her one at a time. She turned back toward Zane and reached out for the last dog. Movement caught her eye. Her eyes grew wide as her brain registered what she was seeing. Kevin was running toward Zane. His arm was extended, and he was pointing...*Gun, behind you.* She screamed the words in her mind.

Zane spun around and threw the knife, embedding it into Kevin's heart. Kevin looked down at his chest as the gun slipped out of his grip. He dropped to his knees and glared at Zane as his body crumpled to the ground.

"I believe we've overstayed our welcome," Rob said as Zane slammed the door. They pulled out, followed by the other two vehicles.

"Is Stan looking after the two trainers?" Blair asked as she pulled supplies from the first aid kit to take care of Zane's wound. At first Blair thought Rob didn't hear her.

"No. The trainers are gone," Rob said.

"Did you look in all the rooms? He probably moved them together to keep a close eye on them."

"I looked everywhere, Blair. I even radioed Stan to help look. He and I searched the facility. There was no sign of them. I'm sorry."

"You think he moved them?" Blair watched Rob closely.

"Anything's possible. All I know is they weren't on site."

"Tell me the truth." She shoved her fisted hands

into her pockets. "They're dead. You think they're both dead, don't you?"

She looked at each of the men. Her unanswered question hung heavy in the air.

CHAPTER ELEVEN

BLAIR WAS RELIEVED when they finally pulled into the Kelly Ranch. The Kelly brothers lived in a lovely two-story, sprawling farmhouse with a view of Puget Sound. The door to the house swung open and Hope bolted from the house taking the four stairs in one leap. She whined as she danced around Blair, her short tail moving so quickly it was a red blur. Blair's mom, Nic, and Jamie walked out behind Hope.

"Blair! I was so worried about you. I can't tell you how happy I am to see you." Blair met her mom halfway and they threw themselves into each other's arms.

"I'm okay, Mom." Blair looked over her mother's shoulder and smiled at Nic. "Thank you for taking care of Hope and for bringing Mom out here."

Blair pulled away and addressed the group of men standing around her. "I'm so grateful for everyone's help. It wouldn't have been possible for me to get the dogs out on my own. I'm in your debt. And especially to you Jamie, for flying out to San Francisco and bringing my mother back with you."

"Let's leave the dogs out here for a while so they can burn off some energy," Zane said. "They've been cooped up for a couple days."

"They'll be okay on their own?" Blair asked.

"They will," Jamie said. "Our ranch is completely fenced in. They can't get out and our ex-special forces friends are here on the ranch to provide security. The dogs are free to run and come into the house when they tire."

"I don't know about anyone else, but I could use a drink right now," Zane said as he took Blair's hand and headed inside.

"Have you uncovered any information about the missing trainers or Pete Baker?" Blair asked as she handed Nic a glass.

"I've been on it since Rob updated me," Nic

said. "No one has seen or heard from Baker. My best guess is that he's gone underground. As far as the two trainers, the story floating around is that they were in Aspen for the weekend skiing. They went down a run that had been closed due to avalanche conditions. They haven't been found, but it's assumed that the pair got swept away. No one has seen them in days. I'm sorry, Blair. It appears you are the only surviving trainer."

"You know that's a cover story; Baker probably killed them. He needs to pay for what he's done. Someone needs to stop him." Blair's chest tightened. She hadn't gotten to know the other two trainers, nonetheless, she wished she could have worked out a plan to get them out when she and Hope escaped.

"Don't worry. He's on our radar. We'll take him down. Just not today," Nic said.

"Then when?" Blair couldn't believe Baker might get away with murder and all the other terrible things he'd done. Where was the justice for all the trainers?

"When we have concrete evidence of his nefarious dealings," Rob said.

"You do. Me! For God's sake. I'm a witness."

"No," Zane and her mom said.

"Don't even think about it, Blair." Zane took both of her hands and seared her with a scorching stare. "You're a loose end and Baker is painfully aware of the fact you're still breathing. Even though you never actually saw him kill anyone, you are a threat to him."

"Zane's right, Blair," Nic said. "The time will come when you'll be an asset to taking Baker down. This isn't that time. It does, however, bring up a particularly important issue."

"Which is?" Blair demanded.

"You and your mom's safety. You realize you can't go back to your old life? At least not yet. You wouldn't survive a week before you both had unfortunate accidents," Nic said.

"Are you telling me I've lived through this terrible nightmare only to have to forfeit my life?" A chill scurried across her shoulders. "My life is about training dogs. I need to get back home and back to work."

Zane laid his hand on her shoulder. Had he seen

the shiver even though she'd thought it went unnoticed?

"Nic's not saying this is forever, but for now you and your mom's safety is our first priority." Zane searched her face looking for her answer.

Blair ran a hand through her hair and chewed on her lip. She looked at her mom. What had she done? Not only had she ruined her own life, she'd dragged her mom into her mess. She dropped her head back and closed her eyes. A small, warm hand covered hers. Blair opened her eyes. Her mom was smiling at her as if she didn't have a care in the world.

"Jamie has been a wonderful host. He and Zane have offered to let us stay here with them until that terrible man is thrown in jail," her mom said. "I like it here, Blair. There's so much to do and I have someone to cook for again."

"Mrs. Sellick is a great cook," Jamie said as he rubbed his stomach. "I've had to increase my exercise time so I can enjoy it all."

Her mom tsked at Jamie as she shook her head.

"I mean, *Cora* is an amazing cook," Jamie corrected himself.

Blair looked around at the people in the room. She had to admit, they'd only recently come into her life, and yet she somehow couldn't picture her life without them.

"Before you say anything there's lots to be done here. And we've brought in sixteen dogs that could really use your care. You can continue to train them. At least until after the holidays, I'd say you're right where you should be," Zane said.

"The dogs." Blair intended to keep them, so they'd need a story. "I overheard conversations between the employees that were assigned to the dogs. Baker bought them from a puppy mill, and he hadn't bothered to fill out any paperwork on them. He was certain no one would challenge him. Pete Baker is an arrogant jackass and with luck he will get what he deserves. With all the trainers gone and Baker nowhere to be found, we can keep them. We can get them all licensed and if anyone asks, we'll tell them they were abandoned."

"Sounds like a plan to me," Nic said. "We're the only ones who know the truth."

BLAIR WAS STARTING to get comfortable at the Kelly Ranch. The brothers had given her and her mom their own individual suites. They told her that their parents had loved to entertain and had built the suites after the boys left. She was settling into a routine, going out to the barn to take the dogs for walks and training them every day.

"This is a great barn." She flashed Zane a smile. She was sitting in a chair and Ace and Dawn had pushed their way next to her, one on each side. Blair laughed and rubbed their sides. "Did your parents have dogs? Those kennels are wonderful."

"We had a few dogs, but it was because of me. When I left, dad spent most of his time with the horses," Zane said. "I've been watching you working the dogs. They all show promise."

"They're great. I'd like to continue training them. They would make excellent service dogs. Would you help me?"

She stood up and walked over to Zane. He was leaning against the wall, petting Sin, who had become Zane's shadow over the past couple of weeks. She'd delayed asking Zane because she was afraid he still wasn't ready to train dogs again. He might never be. Even so, Sin was sneaking into Zane's heart. He may not notice it yet, but it was clear to Blair. Sin had claimed Zane as his own.

"Blair—"

"Please think about it before you say no." Blair rested her hand on his chest. "You're a real natural when it comes to dogs, Zane Kelly. I've never met anyone as good as you. It would be a shame not to use your talents."

"I'll give it some thought." Zane scrubbed his chin with a hand. "Let's take them out for a walk."

Sixteen heads popped up, ears perked. Blair and Zane laughed at the reaction.

"Come on guys." Zane chuckled as all the dogs ran to the door.

ZANE WALKED INTO the den and found his brother working on his laptop and Dawn and Ace stretched out by the fire. Sin went over to join the other dogs.

"Where's Cora?" Zane asked Jamie. He was still

having a difficult time calling Blair's mom by her first name, but she insisted as long as she was living in their house, she was to be called Cora.

"She went up to her suite," Jamie said. "I told her not to overdo with making the Christmas cookies. It made no difference. Have you seen all the varieties? And she says that she's just getting started." Jamie shook his head and smiled. "It was Thanksgiving only two days ago and she is already baking. She plans to make baskets for all the guys. Not that I'm complaining one bit. Where's Blair?"

"She and Hope went to the barn to check on the other dogs. She told me she'd like to continue training the dogs."

Jamie stopped typing and looked up at him.

"I'm not surprised. It's her passion. She reminds me of you. What did you tell her?"

"I didn't. She told me to think about it."

"You've been home for three weeks. You still haven't settled in. You know you have to stay here until the threat of Pete Baker is history, right? That means no taking off for your boat or wherever."

"Do you really think I'd do that?" Zane felt a

pang of hurt. Except, if he were being honest with himself, it was a twinge of guilt. That was his pattern. He'd up and take off whenever the restlessness overcame him.

Jamie raised an eyebrow and studied his brother. "I've known you your entire life and I love you. You know that. Nevertheless, when you get itchy you bolt. All I'm saying is think long and hard before you make any stupid moves. I've seen the way you and Blair are together. I've never seen you like this. If you walk away from her bro, you're a total jackass. She's the one."

Zane dropped into a chair and sighed. "I really am an asshole, aren't I? I walked away from this place when I knew you needed my help. I've run away from any hint of a long-term relationship. I don't want to screw this up."

"Then think before you bolt. This is your home. You've found the missing piece in your life. She's right in front of you. Don't mess it up. Take it from me. It will eat you from the inside out if you do."

"I've been thinking. You haven't done anything with that barn. What would you think if we remodeled it into a state-of-the-art dog training facility? Blair wants to train service dogs. I think I'd enjoy working with her."

"Go for it. You have my blessing." Jamie smiled at him. "That reminds me, Blaze and Cole asked if they could stay. Neither one of them left anything or anyone behind and they like it here. They offered to pay rent. I told them we'd work something out long-term, but for now room and board are on us."

"You think they'd be interested in handling the security for the ranch full-time? With Blair and Mrs. Sellick staying for the time being and the possibility of Blair and I starting up the new business, I'm sure we could keep them busy."

Jamie cocked up one side of his mouth. Zane really had missed his brother.

"I think that's a great idea. And Nic said they'd like to offer the two a contract every now and then. They're still thinking about it. Right now, the ranch is their concern."

"It's great to have guys we can count on," Zane said.

"I agree. And with regard to your business, I'll

bet you could get Bolton's Soldiers to be a backer. Maybe work out a deal with them and provide their PTSD veterans with companions for emotional support along with any other service dogs they might need."

"Are you telling me Bolton's Soldiers already know of some PTSD and other vets in need of service dogs? I haven't been good at staying in contact with the Bolton brothers. That's all on me. I know. Both Nic and Rob have texted me and left tons of messages. I hadn't reached out. The night Rob found me on my boat was the first time I'd seen him in over a year."

"I know."

Jamie quietly studied him. It made Zane uneasy. Jamie was the one person on this earth he couldn't bullshit. His brother knew him best. It had been that way since they were kids.

"There are vets that contract with Bolton's Soldiers," Jamie said as he shut his computer and reached for his beer. "They are great about bringing them on board. Giving them a job, camaraderie, a place to call home, and a reason to live. Some of them can only work support. You know, computer guys, engineers, equipment specialists. That kinda thing but not field work. Bolton's Soldiers have a huge pipeline, Zane. You may not want to work for them, but they could be a great resource for you and Blair's business."

CHAPTER TWELVE

B LAIR WALKED INTO the kitchen and found it full of people. She hadn't seen her mother this happy in years. She was flourishing on the ranch, preparing three meals a day for not only Jamie, Zane, and herself, but for all the other guys staying there.

"Good morning, sweetheart," her mom called over her shoulder.

"Good morning, Mom. Full house today." Blair leaned in and kissed her mom's cheek as she stood over the stove scrambling eggs.

"I was just asking the boys if someone could go and get us a couple of trees," she said. "They actually cut down their own trees. Doesn't that sound wonderful?"

"It does." Blair smiled and took the plate her

mom handed her. Zane pulled out the chair next to him and Blair sat.

"I offered our services." Zane wriggled his eyebrows at her. "We'll take a snowmobile up to the edge of our fence line and head out the back gate. The forest is dense up there and goes on forever."

"That sounds like fun. When are we heading out?"

"I thought we'd go right after the dogs are fed and taken care of. We're expecting another storm later and I'd like us to be back before it starts."

"Zane, take a couple of the guys with you," Jamie suggested.

"I'm free today," Blaze said through a mouthful of eggs. He poked his elbow into the guy sitting next to him.

"What?" Cole stammered. He pinched his eyebrows together and glanced over at Blaze while still balancing a stack of food on his fork, midway between his plate and mouth.

"What do ya mean what? You got bacon in your ears?" Blaze asked. "Zane needs a couple lookouts today. You been bitching about wanting to try out those snowmobiles."

"Oh. Yeah. Count me in, Zane," Cole responded a nanosecond before shoving the fork into his mouth.

"ARE YOU READY to go?" Zane asked.

Cole and Blaze readied three snowmobiles—filled the tanks, checked the engines, and stowed all their supplies, including newly added, easily accessible holders for their loaded Glock 19s. The guys sat on their snowmobiles locked and loaded. Both of them had rifles slung over their shoulders.

Blair put her hands on her hips. "Where's mine?"

"You're riding with me. That way we can talk. It's gonna be difficult to hear when these babies are all humming," Zane said.

"Who's he kidding? It's so you can cuddle up to him," Blaze said. He threw her a wink.

Blair quirked up one side of her mouth. "Well Blaze, I guess I could ride with you instead."

"If only I'd found you first." Blaze bowed his head at Blair and blew Zane a kiss.

"Good answer." Zane squinted until his eyes were slits. He shook his head a couple times feigning annoyance, then turned toward Blair. "You ever drive a snowmobile?"

"I've never even been this close to one. But how hard can they be? I'd love to learn one day soon."

"These aren't your Nana's snowmobiles." Cole caressed the sleek red cowling. "These babies can go over a hundred miles per hour."

"Ignore them," Zane said as he handed her a helmet. "If you speak into this," he said, pointing to the tiny mic woven into the chin strap, "I'll hear you. And only me."

They started the engines and headed for the back of the ranch. It was a beautiful day and Blair soaked in the scenery. They reached the gate. Zane pushed a button on the dashboard and opened it. When the last snowmobile cleared the gate it automatically closed. As they got out into the forest, the two guys split off widening the distance between them.

"Where are they going?" Blair asked.

"They're making sure we're the only ones out

here. We'll hear their vehicles, but probably won't see them again until we start back for the house."

"You mean they're not helping us cut down the trees?"

"Nope. Just you and me."

Blair snugged up against Zane's back. Her thighs pressed into his, much like the rider on a motorcycle. He reached down with his gloved hand and rubbed his hand up and down her leg. Sparks of heat snapped everywhere his hand made contact. He slowed the machine and cruised through the trees.

"Let me know when that perfect Christmas tree jumps out at you. I'm heading up the mountain to an area where I've seen a few that I think will work. But if you find one you like, just point it out."

Blair took in the breathtaking landscape and the wonderful scent of evergreens. She could ride with Zane all day and be perfectly content. He drove for a few more minutes and stopped.

"This is the place." Zane pointed ahead to a denser grouping of trees. "Shall we go take a look?" He helped her off the snowmobile and removed his helmet. He slid the duffle he'd slung over his chest to his back. "So, Cora wants a big tree for the living room and a smaller one. She didn't tell me where she planned to put the smaller one."

"You never can tell what Mom is planning. Oh, this one is beautiful." Blair ran her hands over the branches.

"This was one of my picks. It's a blue spruce. I'd say it fits the bill for the big tree." Zane looked at Blair. "What do you think? Should we cut or keep looking?"

"I think it's perfect. Let's cut."

"I love a woman who knows what she wants." He pulled the bag off and dropped it on the ground.

Blair laughed. She stopped when Zane smiled at her. She could feel the heat from his body, and he was standing at least a foot away. He closed the distance as if he—read her mind? Instantly his smile turned wickedly sexy. He stepped into her, placed his hands on her cheeks and claimed her lips. His heat poured into her. Blair wrapped her arms around him drawing him closer.

The first flakes of snow fell, landed on them, and

sizzled into steam. Zane pulled back and looked at her.

"We'd better get our trees while we still have time." He kissed her again. Then he stepped away, grabbed the bag, and pulled out a saw, rope, and a tightly folded tarp. "I'll cut the tree. It's your job to hold the tree up, so that it doesn't fall on me."

Blair took hold of the tree as Zane cut it down. He took the trunk out of her hands and dragged the tree to the ground. He unfolded the tarp, and the two of them rolled the tree onto it. Then he quickly wrapped the tarp around the tree and secured it with a rope.

"Let's go pick out our second one. We'll get this on the way back through."

They wandered through the trees chatting and holding hands. It wasn't long before they picked out and cut down their second tree. They repeated the same process as the first. Within minutes Zane grabbed the rope that was attached to the base of the tree. He dragged the tree behind them as they headed back for their first tree.

Three shots rang out through the forest. Zane

grabbed Blair, threw her to the ground, and blanketed her with his body, pushing her deep into the snow. Two more shots pierced the silence. Zane pulled out his phone and pushed a button.

"Damnit, Cole. Answer your phone." He disconnected and hit another button. "Blaze, what's going on? Is it Baker's people?" Zane listened to the man on the other end. "And you're sure? Okay. We'll meet up with you where we split off. Contact me if anything changes."

"Who's shooting?" Blair asked as he stuffed his phone back into his pocket.

"A couple of idiot hunters. They're on posted private property and they took a shot at Cole thinking he was a deer. Dumb shits."

"Is Cole okay?"

"Yeah. Seems their shooting skills are as bad as their reading skills. They can't do either worth a damn. They missed Cole by a mile. Blaze said Cole scared the shit out of them. Told them if they ever stepped foot on the property again, he'd hunt them down and tie them to a tree and leave them for the bears to eat."

"The owner of this property doesn't mind you taking their trees?"

"Nope. We take at least one every year and re-plant new trees to replace the ones we take. These last few years, I've cut down trees I planted as a kid."

"Just who owns this property?"

"The Kellys." Zane chuckled. Blair punched him in the arm. "Ouch."

He rubbed his arm pretending to be in pain. She rolled her eyes and shook her head at his pitiful act.

When they reached the first tree, Zane grabbed some more rope from his bag and tied the two trees together. He dragged them over to the snowmobile and tied them to the back.

Blair started to shiver. When Zane knocked her down, snow had gone down her neck, as well as into her boots.

"You're shivering, Blair. We need to get you back." Zane got on the snowmobile and Blair climbed on behind him. "Wrap your arms tightly around me and scoot up as close as you can. It will keep you warmer."

She did as he suggested and rested her cheek

against his back. The snow was falling harder. The storm was here to stay. The clouds filled the sky, blocking out the sun and the late morning looked more like dusk. Zane switched on his headlights. They quickly caught up to Cole and Blaze and headed to the warmth of the house.

"GET BLAIR INSIDE," Blaze said as soon as they arrived. "Her lips are blue. We'll take care of the snowmobiles and the trees."

"Thanks, guys." Zane helped Blair into the house.

They pulled off their wet boots and coats in the kitchen. Zane picked up a note sitting on the counter. "Jamie and two of the guys took your mom to town. I thought the house sounded quiet." Blair's teeth were chattering. Her clothes were soaked. "Come on. You need a hot shower, then I'll make you a hot buttered rum."

ZANE WALKED BLAIR toward her suite, then stopped

at the door to his room, opened it, and led her in. He walked her into his bathroom and turned on the hot water tap in his oversized shower. Six shower heads sprayed hot water, instantly steaming up the room.

"Get in the shower and I'll go get you the drink."

She tried to unbutton her shirt, but her hands wouldn't stop shaking. Zane gently brushed her hands away and unbuttoned it. He pulled off her shirt and the soaked turtleneck underneath. Then he slid down her jeans and carefully peeled off her long underwear, leaving her standing in her black satin matching panties and bra. Still squatting in front of her he couldn't help but run his gaze up over her. Blair was perfection. He didn't touch her as he stood and yet every inch of her called to him. It was all he could do not to grab her and trace every millimeter with his hands. Better yet—his lips.

Zane sighed and led her to the shower, and she stood under the shower heads, her face turned up to the ceiling. The water cascaded down her body and streamed down her straight, midnight-black hair. The sight of her was intoxicating, Zane could swear he heard her essence sing out to him. He was drawn to her, like a bumble bee to a newly blossomed flower. Sparks flashed in his vision. Fully clothed, he stepped in behind her and unhooked her bra. He slid his hands down her bra straps, reveling in the satiny sensation of her skin. He leaned in and kissed the back of her neck. Blair turned into his arms. She dragged his head toward her and kissed him. As he lifted her off her feet, she wrapped her elegant legs tightly around his. His low growl escaped his lips and vibrated between them.

A couple of hours later they were still tangled in each other's arms lying on Zane's bed.

"Didn't you promise me a hot buttered rum?" Blair teased as she traced her finger over the outline of his pecs.

"That was before you distracted me." Zane's phone rang and he grabbed it off the nightstand. "Hey, Jamie. How's it going?" Zane listened for a few minutes. "Do you want the guys to come and get you? Okay. Take your time and be careful."

"What's going on?" Blair asked.

"The storm is worse than first expected. They're

still in town waiting for the snowplows to clear the roads before heading back up here. It could be a couple of hours." While quickly raising his eyebrows up and down, Zane asked, "now, what was that about something hot and buttered?"

CHAPTER THIRTEEN

T HE FOLLOWING WEEKS passed quickly. Between working with the dogs and helping her mom get the house ready for Christmas, the days flew by. But no matter how busy their days, Zane and Blair spent every night together, sneaking into each other's rooms and leaving in the wee hours like they were high school kids.

It was Christmas Eve, and everyone was helping clean up after dinner. They moved into the spacious family room, joined by all the dogs. Most nights the guys and Jamie would take a dog or two for the night. Blair thought it was good for the dogs to be split up and spend time with different people. But the four Dobermans that Blair and Zane claimed as their own stayed with them.

Everyone sat around the tree enjoying drinks

and telling stories. Cora served them her favorite baked Alaska made from scratch. The cake layer was homemade brownies with a layer of cherry ice cream and a layer of salted caramel ice cream. All topped with a toasted golden marshmallow meringue.

"Oh. My. God! I'm in heaven," Cole exclaimed between huge mouthfuls of the decadent dessert.

"I'm in love...will you marry me, Cora?" Blaze asked holding out his empty plate in hopes for another piece.

Everyone's spoons froze. They gawked at Blaze and then at the flustered look on Cora's face. They all erupted in laughter. After they all laughed themselves out, Zane looked around the room, cocked his head, and smiled.

"What's up?" Jamie asked his brother.

"It's been a long time since this house has held this much laughter," Zane said.

"Welcome home, Zane." Jamie patted him on the back.

Zane's phone buzzed.

"It's Nic. I need to talk to him. I'll be right back."

He kissed Blair on her forehead as he left the room.

"THIS MUST BE important if you're calling on Christmas Eve," Zane said.

"I was hoping you'd call me. Since I haven't heard from you, I decided to make the first move," Nic said. "Have you given any thought to becoming a full-time contractor with us? We could sure use your skills."

"I have. I won't come to work with you full-time. However, if you need me every now and then I'll do my best to help."

"What are you planning on doing with yourself?"

"I'm building Blair a new dog training facility. My priority will be the dog business. Her goal is to continue training service dogs, especially PTSD trained dogs that help our veterans and improve their quality of life. We'll also serve the private industry, but the military is our main focus."

"That's fantastic, Zane. We'd be interested in speaking with you both. Maybe we could assist you financially. It would be great if down the road we could use your dogs on missions."

"I'll need to run it by Blair, but it sounds doable. We'll invite you out for a visit as soon as we have the facility built and give you the tour and more details regarding our plans. Have you made any progress locating Baker?"

"Nothing yet. We're running down every lead. Baker has connections everywhere, and the mafia is his family. I'll let you know the second we come up with anything."

"That's about the same here. My FBI contact was here a couple of weeks ago. Blair told him her story. He's been running down her leads, but so far, none of the trainers that died can be directly connected to Pete Baker or his company."

"How can that be?" Nic asked. "I don't care how good you are; someone had to see something."

"Problem is there have been two or more witnesses at every scene. Every one of them swears they never laid eyes on Baker or any of his associates at the crime scene."

"It makes me wonder what kind of hold he has on all those witnesses," Nic said.

"You and me both."

"Sounds like this is gonna be a long game. If your friends need to leave, I'm sure we can work out some long-term security. You must maintain constant vigilance. The first time you let down your guard you and I know damn well Pete Baker will use it as his opportunity to grab or kill Blair."

"I have no intention of letting my guard down. I know Baker is a sadistic bastard. Blaze and Cole are staying here for good. I've talked with my other three friends. They're happy to stay, but I told them to let me know if their plans change and they need to take off. Thanks for the offer, Nic. We have it handled. I'll let you know if anything changes."

"Good," Nic said. "I won't keep you any longer. Tell everyone Merry Christmas."

ZANE REJOINED THE group. They'd become a family and he liked the feel of it. As the night wore on, the group thinned down until only Zane, Blair, Ace, Dawn, Sin, and Hope were left. Zane got up and pulled a long tube with a bow from behind the tree.

"This is for you." Zane handed the tube to Blair.

"I want you to open it now."

Blair pulled off one end of the tube and dumped a roll of paper into her lap. Her eyebrows pinched together as she picked up the paper and looked at it.

"What is this?" she asked.

"You'll have to open it up and see."

SHE WATCHED THE mischief in his eyes. What was he up to? She unrolled the paper. Across the top was written Blair's Training Facility. The drawing detailed the entire layout of a brand-new dog training center.

"You're building me a new training facility?" She couldn't believe what she was seeing.

"I am. A state-of-the-art training facility. Nothing is set in stone. We don't hammer a single nail until you give your approval. And you'll need to come up with a name for your business."

"What about Jamie? He already has to put up with my mom and me until Baker is found. Having a business on your property would mean I'd be here forever. I won't intrude on your ranch if Jamie disapproves."

"Jamie enjoys having you and Cora here. He says it gives the old place the life it used to have before we lost our parents. We talked about the training facility weeks ago. He thinks it's a great idea. Especially if it means I'll be staying on the ranch."

"And will you?" Blair held her breath, her eyes locked on his, and waited quietly for his answer.

"For as long as you do." He gave her one of his gorgeous smiles and his eyes twinkled.

"I absolutely love it. But I'll only agree to it under one condition. I want us to be partners."

"Deal," Zane said. "Let's roll this out on the dining table, and I'll explain some of my ideas."

"I LOVE IT," Blair said after he finished going over the plans.

"It's just some preliminary thoughts. I figured the two of us would put on the final touches."

"I've been wondering," Blair started, "what would you think of housing our potential clients while we taught them and the dogs. They will have to build a relationship and work as a team. That may take some time. I thought we could put together a detailed program and use it as our foundation."

"I like where you're going." Zane pointed to the far side of the ranch. "We have this large area here that hasn't been used in years. It would be a perfect place to build a dormitory, or a grouping of small cabins."

"It would mean we'd have to hire employees. Housekeepers and cooks at the very least." Blair stood back and looked at the layout again. "That's probably not feasible in the beginning. We won't have a large budget."

"Don't take your idea off the table just yet. I have some money put away," Zane said.

"I can't ask you to contribute more than I can," she said.

"We'll work it out. Nic and Rob Bourne are interested in our plans. They've offer to be a backer if we're looking for one. They would also like to talk to us about providing their vets with service dogs, and possibly use them on missions when needed. So, we have some options."

"I think those are wonderful ideas."

Zane wrapped his arm around her. "We can sleep on it. Right now, I'd like a drink, how about you?"

"I have something for you first," Blair said. "I was hoping to have something special for you, Zane. Unfortunately, yesterday I learned it didn't work out the way I'd hoped. Let's sit down."

They sat down on the sofa. There was a lump in Blair's throat that felt like the size of a softball. She swallowed and tried to clear her throat. Her hands began to tremble, but she had to hold herself together for him.

"What's wrong, Blair? Is it all too much, too soon? Are you having second thoughts about the facility? You and your mom are welcome to stay no matter what. The ranch is the safest place for the both of you." Worry creased his forehead.

"I know. And I'm not having second thoughts. I'm giddy about our plans." She rubbed her hand over one of his.

"This isn't about me. I have a good friend from my college days that works for Veterinarians Without Borders. She's been with them for years. When I first arrived here, I contacted her and told her about Axel. It just so happened she was on her way to drop off supplies in Bosnia and visit some of the villages. She has a few vet friends there that she likes to check up on. She promised me she'd find out what she could. I'd given up hope when I hadn't heard from her, until yesterday. After you left to run errands, Jamie and Blaze drove me into town. My friend made a stopover at SeaTac on her way back home. Cole went to the airport and picked her up.

"She said that while she was in Bosnia, she heard a story about a military dog left for dead. One of the locals brought him into town and took him over to the vet. He was in bad shape, Zane." Blair swiped at the stray tear that threatened to slip down her cheek. "My friend told me they did everything they could for him, but in the end, he didn't make it. I'm so sorry."

"How do they know for sure it was Axel. How does your friend know for certain what they told her was a true story?"

Blair could feel Zane's pain. He bottled it up deep down inside, except that didn't stop it from spilling into her mind. She stood up and walked over to the Christmas tree and pulled out a small, wrapped box that was nestled in the branches. She walked back to the sofa and sat down next to Zane and handed the box to him. He stared at the box for so long, Blair began to think she should've just let it alone. She reached out to take the box back, and Zane laid his hand over hers.

Zane moved her hand to his thigh. Then he removed the lid and stared down at a leather collar he knew so well. The ID tag was attached. On the inside, chiseled into the collar, it said Axel.

"My friend was given his collar. At first, she was just planning to tell me what happened to Axel. Only the longer she thought about it, the more she felt you needed closure. I'm sincerely sorry, Zane."

"Your friend was right." He looked at Blair and she saw wetness brimming his eyes. "I'm thankful to you for everything you did to find Axel. You got me the answers the military wouldn't. Thank you, Blair.

Losing Axel was excruciating."

Zane ran the collar through his hands. "It was impossible for me to see my future because I could barely make it through each day. But losing him meant I was here when this mission needed me. Axel's gift to me was bringing you into my life and giving me a new cause and future with you." He leaned into her and placed a gentle kiss on her lips.

"Let's all go to bed." Blair stood up and reached out for his hand.

"Do you want to take the dogs or should I?" Zane asked.

"We're all going to sleep in the same room and tomorrow morning we're all waking up in that room. I don't want to spend another morning wishing you were lying next to me. This is our first Christmas, and we should share it together."

Zane took her into his arms. "That sounds perfect to me. But are you ready for the entire gang to know about us?" He held his breath as he waited for her answer.

"I have a very strong feeling they already know." Blair smiled up at him.

"I can't recall a time in my life when I was as happy as I am at this moment. Merry Christmas, Blair."

"Merry Christmas, Zane." She took both of his hands in hers and stood on her tippy toes to kiss him on the cheek. Then she wrapped her arm around his waist. Zane snugged her into him, wrapping his arm around her shoulders. She nestled into him. Her head against the solid warmth of his chest as they walked toward his room together.

Also by the Author

Miss Demeanor, P.I.
P.I.~I Love You, Book 1
Twice As Bad, Book 2

Hunters & Seekers
Salvaging Truth, Book 1

The Winters Sisters
Chasing Victory, Book One
Payton's Pursuit, Book Two
Willow's Discovery, Book Three
Corralling Kenzie, Book Four

Forever Christmas In Glenville
Christmas Reflections, Book One
Christmas Ivy, Book Two
Christmas Chemistry, Book Three

Love, Take Two
Love's Always Paws-Able
Building Up to Love
Uncharted Love

YOU CAN FIND JOANNE HERE

Email: joannejaytanie@wavecable.com

Website: www.joannejaytanie.com

About The Author

Joanne writes romantic suspense, mystery/thriller/ suspense, paranormal, and contemporary romance. A transplant from upstate New York, Joanne lives with her husband and Doberman in their home located on the Olympic Peninsula with a panoramic view of the Olympic Mountains.

When she's not writing, she loves to travel and enjoys time with her family and friends. Joanne has recently returned to dog training. Mazie, their newest addition to the family, loves to work. The duo is learning Scent Work and plans to start trialing in 2021.

In her previous life, Joanne showed and titled dogs in conformation, obedience, agility, and rally. She has worked in personnel, finance and managed her husband's forensic engineering firm.

Joanne is a PAN member of Romance Writers of America, Kiss of Death, Greater Seattle Romance Writers Chapter, Rose City Romance Writers, Sisters In Crime, Fantasy, Futuristic & Paranormal, and Pacific NW Writers Association. She served as President of Peninsula Romance Writers, which was Debbie Macomber's home chapter.

Made in the USA
Coppell, TX
08 June 2021